I0660157

The Heart of Old Hickory
and
Other Stories of Tennessee

By

Will Allen Dromgoole
[1860-1934]

Preface by B.O. Flower

THE HEART OF OLD HICKORY AND OTHER STORIES OF TENNESSEE

BY

WILL ALLEN DROMGOOLE

WITH PREFACE BY B. O. FLOWER

SECOND EDITION

BOSTON
ESTES AND LAURIAT PUBLISHERS

To My Father John Easter Dromgoole

CONTENTS.

PREFACE

ONE day in the summer of 1890 I received a manuscript entitled "Fiddling His Way to Fame," accompanied by a brief note. Both were signed Will Allen Dromgoole. I read the sketch, and at once remarked to Mrs. Flower that, in my judgment, this was a case of the hand of Esau and the voice of Jacob, or, in other words, though the name signed was that of a man, the sketch was certainly the work of a woman or had been recast by a woman. There were certain fine strokes and delicate touches, in a word, a general atmosphere evincing a fine interior appreciation of the working of the human heart which characterizes woman's thought at its best and which stamped this as the work of a woman. I know this view does not accord with the opinion held by many of my friends in regard to mental differentiation, but my experience thoroughly convinces me that there is a subtle quality and intuitional power which is distinctly characteristic of woman, though there are men who possess this subtle something in a more or less marked degree.

I immediately accepted the sketch, as it was something I wanted to lighten the pages of my review, and because it possessed a certain charm which is rare among modern writers, being humorous and pathetic by turns, wonderfully true to life, and yet free from the repulsive elements so often present in realistic sketches.

Since that day the brilliant little Tennessee authoress, who bears a man's name, but who is one of the most womanly of women, has contributed more fiction to the **ARENA** than any other writer. Her sketches have proved extremely popular, owing to her artistic skill in bringing out the pathos and humor of the situations depicted, no less than the fidelity with which she draws her characters and her intense sympathy with humble life. She constantly reminds the reader of Charles Dickens, although her writings are free from the tendency to caricature and overdraw which always seems to me to be present in the works of the great English author.

Miss Dromgoole is nothing if not a Southerner, and her love of the South is only surpassed by the affection she feels for the mountains and valleys of her dear old Tennessee. She is a woman of conviction and possesses the spirit of our era in a large degree. No one familiar with her work during the past four years can fail to note how steadily her views have broadened and how rapidly popular prejudice has given place to that broad and justice-loving spirit which is so needed in modern life, and which enables its possessor to rise above petty prejudice or unreasoning conventionalism when conscience speaks to the soul.

Miss Dromgoole has had a hard life in more ways than one. It has been a constant struggle. It was not until after the death of her mother, who had ever encouraged and believed in her, that she began to write for the public. That was about nine years ago. With the death of her mother the home was broken up, and the loss of the dearest friend and counsellor to a nature so intense as hers, and the necessity of earning a living, led her to carry out her mother's oft-expressed wish and write for publication. Her first ambitious attempt won a prize offered by the Youth's Companion, and that journal and other publications accepted many of her stories. "But," to quote from her own words, "it was not until 'Fiddling His Way to Fame' appeared in the **ARENA** that I suddenly found myself famous, and since then I have had more orders for work than I have been able to fill."

As the personality of a famous writer is always interesting, I propose to give a brief descriptive sketch of the little woman of whom the South has just reason to be proud before speaking of this book. She is small of stature, fragile in appearance, intense in her nature, and of a highly-strung nervous organism. I seldom care to dwell on the ancestry of an individual, as I think that sort of thing has been greatly overdone, and I believe with Bulwer that "not to the past but to the future looks true nobility, and finds its blazon in posterity." And yet the ancestry of an individual may sometimes prove a helpful and interesting study. I have frequently noticed in the writings of authors who exhibit great versatility, no less than in the lives of individuals who seem to present strikingly contradictory phases of character, the explanation of these phenomena in their ancestry. In the case of Miss Dromgoole we find an interesting illustration of this nature. Her great-grandfather Edward Dromgoole emigrated from Sligo, Ireland; as he had accepted the tenets of Protestantism and his people were strong Catholics, it was unpleasant for him to longer remain in his native land. He became a prominent pioneer Methodist minister in Virginia. One of his sons, a well-known orator, represented the Petersburg district in congress. Her maternal grandfather was of Danish extraction, while her great-grandmother on her father's side was an Englishwoman, and her great-grandfather on the mother's side married a French lady. Here we have the mingling of Irish, Danish, English, and French blood, with some striking characteristics of each of these peoples appearing perceptibly in the person and works of Miss Dromgoole. Though she repudiates the English * in her blood, her sturdy loyalty to high principles and an ethical strength wedded to a certain seriousness, almost sadness,

* In a personal letter Miss Dromgoole says: "I do not know what I am. I claim the Irish and the French. I feel the Danish blood in my veins at times, but the cold blood of the English I repudiate."strongly

suggest the Anglo-Saxon at its best. She has the Irish keen sense of humor, which is seen in her writings and lectures, no less than in her conversation. The energy and determination together with the persistency of the Dane, and some of the bright and versatile characteristics of the French, are evident in her life and work, although there is a strong tendency to dwell too much on the gloomy side of life which even the Irish humor and the cheerful qualities of the French blood have not overcome. This is due I think largely to the blow occasioned by the death of her mother and the terrible struggle which has marked her life, and which has been waged against adversity with much the same sense of loyalty to right as marked the Roundheads in their conflicts with King Charles I.

Her parents, John E. Dromgoole and Rebecca Mildred Blanch, after marriage, moved from Brunswick County, Virginia, to Tennessee. Miss Dromgoole was born in Murfreesboro, in the last-named state, and graduated from the Female Academy of Clarksville, Tennessee. For several years she was engrossing clerk for the senate of Tennessee. During recent years she has spent much of her time in Boston and New York, where she has been warmly welcomed and has many sincere admirers among those who appreciate genius and sterling worth.

The present volume illustrates the author's power and versatility in a forcible manner, and will prove a valuable addition to the literature of genuine merit from the pens of Southern writers. The first sketch, "The Heart of Old Hickory," is, in my judgment, one of the finest short stories of the present generation. It has proved unusually popular, and displays the wonderful power of its gifted author in blending humor and pathos, while investing with irresistible fascination a sketch which, in the hands of any other than an artist, would appear tame and insipid. It is a masterpiece in its way, and like all her writings deals largely with the hopes, sorrows, aspirations, and tragedies of the common life in Tennessee. I think it also will convince all readers that the author might have made a great success as an advocate before a jury had she chosen law instead of literature for her professsion. "Fiddling His Way to Fame" is a unique and most delightful sketch, in which ex-Governor Taylor again figures conspicuously. "A Wonderful Experience Meeting" and "Who Broke Up de Meeting'?" are true to the present-day negro dialect. Unlike many persons who essay this field of literature, Miss Dromgoole never overdoes the dialect, and those familiar with the vernacular as spoken in Tennessee and Kentucky will recognize the absolute fidelity to the requirements which characterizes these amusing and faithful sketches. They are in her happiest vein, and are extremely well written. "Rags" is a pathetic picture of the street-gamin life showing the strength of our author when she paints in sombre hues.

"The Heart of the Woods" is in many respects strikingly unlike the other stories. Through it flows a strain of supernormalism which is rarely found in the writings of our Southern authors. In many ways it is one of Miss Dromgoole's best productions, and illustrates anew the versatility of the author. Perchance the manes of some of her Norse ancestors may have been about her when she penned the sombre but fascinating creation "The Heart of the Woods."

In "Ole Logan's Courtship" we come out again into the sunshine, as here we find humor predominating. This sketch, like most of Miss Dromgoole's short stories, is taken from life. The bases of her best sketches have been actual occurrences, which, however, required the subtle power of the true artist to make others see and feel the life, with its sunshine and shadows, in the scenes depicted. The play of Hamlet, it will be remembered, existed before Shakespeare's time; but it was the immortal bard of the Avon who breathed into it the breath of life, such as comes only from the imagination of a genius, and lo! the mannikin was imbued with life.

In "Christmas Eve at the Corner Grocery" we are strongly reminded of the Dickens quality in the writings of our author, without the slightest suggestion of imitation. This sketch has proved unusually popular as a recitation at Christmas entertainments, and almost ranks with "The Heart of Old Hickory " in popularity with public readers. It is a charming story to be read at any time, but especially appropriate for the holidays.

I believe that this volume will take a high place among the meritorious works of modern Southern authors. Tennessee has just xii reason to be proud of the little authoress who has depicted so many phases of humble life within her borders with such fidelity, such delicacy, and such rare pathos and humor.

B. O. FLOWER.

THE HEART OF OLD HICKORY.

NOISELESSLY, dreamily, with that suggestion of charity which always lingers about a snowstorm, fell the white flakes down, in the arms of the gray twilight. There was an air of desolation about the grim old State House, as, one by one, the great doors creaked the departure of the various occupants of the honorable old pile that overlooks the city and the sluggish sweep of the Cumberland beyond. The last loitering feet came down the damp corridors; the rustle of a woman's skirts sent a kind of ghostly rattle through the shadowy alcoves.

The Governor heard the steps and the rustle of the stiff bombazine skirts, and wondered, in a vague way, why it was that women would work beyond the time they bargained for. The librarian was always the last to leave, except the Governor himself. He had heard her pass that door at dusk, day in, day out, for two years, and always after the others were gone. He never felt quite alone in the empty State House until those steps had passed by. This evening, however, they stopped, and he looked up inquiringly as the knob was carefully turned, and the librarian entered the executive office.

"I only stopped to say a word for the little hunchback's mother," she said. "She is not a bad woman, and her provocation was great. Moreover, she is a woman."

He remembered the words long after the librarian had gone.

"She is a woman." That was a strange plea to advance for a creature sentenced to the gallows. He sighed, and again took up the long roll of paper lying upon his desk.

15

"Inasmuch as she was sorely wronged, beaten, tortured by seeing her afflicted child ill-treated, we, the undersigned, do beg of your excellency all charity and all leniency compatible with the laws of the State, and the loftier law of mercy."

Oh, that was an old story; yet it read well, too, that old, old petition with that old, old plea--charity. Five hundred names were signed to it; and yet, thrice five hundred tongues would lash him if he set his own name there. It was a hard thing,--to hold life in his hand and refuse it. Those old threadbare stories, old as pain itself, had well-nigh wrought his ruin; his political ruin. At least the papers said as much; they had sneeringly nicknamed him "Tenderheart," and compared him, with a sneer, too, to that old sterling hero--the Governor's eyes sought the east window, where the statue of Andrew Jackson loomed like a bronze giant amid the snowflakes and the gathering twilight. They had compared them, the old hero who lived in bronze, and the young human-heart who had no "back-bone," and was moved by a rogue's cry.

Yet, he had loved that majestic old statue since the day he entered the executive office as chief ruler of the State, and had fancied for a moment the old hero was welcoming him into her trust and highest honor, as he sat astride his great steed with his cocked hat lifted from the head that had indeed worn "large honors." But he had been so many times thrust into his teeth, he could almost wish--

"Papers! Papers! wanter paper, mister?"

A thin little face peered in at the door, a face so old, so strangely unchildlike, he wondered for an instant what trick of pain's had fastened that knowing face of a man upon the misshapen body of a child.

"Yes," said the Executive, "I want a Banner."

The boy had bounded forward, as well as a dwarfed foot would allow, at the welcome "Yes," but stopped midway the apartment, and slowly shook his head at the remainder of the sentence, while an expression, part jubilance, part regret, and altogether disgust, crossed his little old-young face.

"Don't sell that sort, mister," said he, "none o' our club don't. It's--low-lived."

The Governor smiled, despite his hard day with the critics and the petition folk.

"What? You don't sell the Evening Banner, the only independent journal in the city?"

The newsboy was a stranger to sarcasm.

"That's about the size on't," he said as he edged himself, a veritable bundle of tatters, a trifle nearer the red coals glowing in the open grate.

Suddenly, the Executive remembered that it was cold. There were ridges of snow on the bronze statue at the window. He noticed, too, the movement of the tatters toward the fire, and with his hand, a very white, gentle-seeming hand it was, motioned the little vagabond toward the grate. No sooner did he see the thin, numb fingers stretched toward the blaze than he remembered the sneers of "the only independent journal." It was not far from right, surely, when it called him "soft-hearted," was this boycotted Banner which the newsboys refused to handle. The Executive smiled; the boycott, at all events, was comical.

"And so," said he, "you refuse to sell the Banner. Why is that?"

"Shucks!" was the reply. " 'Taint no good. None o' us likes it. Yer see, cully--" The Executive started; but a glance at the earnest, unconscious face convinced him the familiarity was not intentional disrespect. "You see," the boy went on, "it sez mean things, tells lies, yer know, about a friend o' mine."

One foot, the shorter, withered member, was thrust dangerously near to the glowing coalbed; the little gossip was making himself thoroughly at home. The Executive observed it, and smiled. He also noted the weary droop of the shoulders, and impulsively pointed to a seat. He only meant something upon which to rest himself, and did not notice, until the tatters dropped wearily into the purple luxuriance, that he had invited the little Arab to a seat in a great, deep armchair of polished cherry, richly upholstered with royal purple plush, finished with a fringe of tawny gold.

Instinctively, he glanced toward the east window. The bronze face wore a solemn, sturdy frown, but on the tip of the great general's cocked hat a tiny sparrow had perched, and stood coquettishly picking at the white snowflakes that fell upon the bronze brim.

"And so the Banner abuses your friend?"

The Executive turned again to the tatters, costly ensconced in the soft depths of the State's purple. The old-young head nodded.

"And what does it say of him?"

He wondered if it could abuse any one quite so soundly and so mercilessly as it had dealt with him.

"Aw, sher!" the tatters, in state, was growing contemptuous. "It called him a 'mugwump.' "

The Governor colored; it had said the same of him.

"An'," the boy went on, "it said ez ther' wa'n't no backbone to him, an' ez he wuz only fitten to set the pris'ners loose, an' to play the fiddle. An' it said a lot about a feller named Ole Poplar--"

"What!"

The smile upon the Governor's lips gave place to a hearty laugh, as the odd little visitor ransacked the everglades of memory for the desired timber from which heroes are hewn.

"Poplar? Ben't it poplar? Naw, cedar,--ash, wonnut, hick'ry--that's it! Hick'ry. Ole Hick'ry. It said a lot about him; an' it made the boys orful mad, an' they won't sell the nasty paper."

The tatters began to quiver with the excitement of the recital. The little old-young face lost something of its patient, premature age while the owner rehearsed the misdoings of the city's independent afternoon journal.

The Executive listened with a smile of amused perplexity. Evidently he was the "friend" referred to, else the journal had said the same of two parties.

"Who is your friend?" he asked vaguely wondering as to what further developments he might expect.

"Aw," said the boy," he ain't my friend perzactly. He's Skinny's though, an' all the boys stan's up for Skinny."

"And who is 'Skinny'?"

A flash of contempt shot from the small, deep-set eyes.

"Say, cully," his words were slow and emphatic, "wher' wuz you raised? Don't you know Skinny?"

The Executive shook his head. "Is he a newsboy?"

"He wuz--" the tatters were still a moment, only a twitch of the lips and a slight, choking movement of the throat told the boy was struggling with his emotions. Then the rough, frayed sleeve was drawn across the bundle of papers strapped across his breast, where a tear glistened upon the front page of the Evening Herald. "He wuz a newsboy--till yistiddy. We buried uv him yistiddy."

The momentary silence was broken only by the soft click of the clock telling the run of time. It was the Governor who spoke then. "And this man whom the Banner abuses was Skinny's friend."

"Yes. This here wuz Skinny's route. I took it yistiddy. Yer see Skinny didn't have no mammy an' no folks, an' no meat onter his bones,--that's why we all named him Skinny. He wuz jest b-o-n-z-e-s. An' ther' wuz nobody ter keep keer uv him when he wuz sick, an' he jest up an' died."

Without the window the snow fell softly, softly. The little brown bird hopped down from the great general's hat and sought shelter in the bronze bosom of his fluted vesture. Poor little snowbird!--the human waif which the newsboys had buried--for him the bronze bosom of Charity had offered no shelter from the storm. The tatters in velvet had forgotten the cold, and the presence before him, as he gazed into the dreamful warmth of the fire. He did not see the motion of the Governor's hand across his eyes, nor did he know how the great man was rehearsing the Banner's criticisms.

"He cannot hear a beggar's tale without growing chicken-hearted and opening the prison doors to every red-handed murderer confined there who can put up a pretty story."

He was soft-hearted; he knew it, and regretted it many times to the bronze general at the window. But this evening there was a kind of defiance about him; he was determined to dare the old warrior-statesman, and the slanderous Banner--and his own "chicken-heart," too.

"Tell me," said he, "about this friend of Skinny's."

"The Gov'ner?"

"Was it the Governor?"

"Say!" Oh, the scorn of those young eyes! "Is ther' anybody else can pardon out convicts? In course 'twuz the Gov'ner. Skinny had a picture uv him, too. A great big un, an' golly! but 'twuz pritty. Kep' it hangin' over his cot what Nickerson, the p'liceman ez ain't got no folks neither, like Skinny, let him set up in a corner o' his room down ter Black Bottom. Say, cully, does you know the Gov'ner?"

"Yes; but go on with your story. Tell me all about Skinny and--his friend!"

The tatters settled back into the purple cushions. The firelight played upon the little old face, and the heat drew the dampness from the worn clothes, enveloping the thin figure in a vapor that might have been a poetic dream-mist but for the ragged reality slowly thawing in the good warmth. The bundle of papers had been lifted from the sunken chest and placed carefully by on the crimson and olive rug, while the human bundle settled itself to tell the story of Skinny.

"Me an' him wuz on the pris'n route," said he, "till--yistiddy. Least I wuz ther till yistiddy. Skinny tuk this route last year. He begged it fur me when he--come ter quit, because I ben't ez strong ez-- Solermun, you know. Wa'n't he the strong un? Solermun or Merthuslem, I git mixed in them bible fellers. But 'twuz when we wuz ter the pris'n route I larnt about Skinny's friend, the Gov'ner, you know. First ther' was ole Jack Nasby up an' got parelized, an' w'an't no 'count ter nobody, let 'lone ter the State. 'A dead expense,' the ward'n said. He suffered orful, too, an' so'd his wife. An' one day Skinny said he wuz goin' ter write a pertition an' git all the 'fishuls ter sign it, an' git the Gov'ner ter pard'n ole Nasby out. They all signed it-- one o' the convic's writ it, but they all told Skinny ez 'twuz no use, 'cause he wouldn't do it. An' one day, don't yer think when ole Nasby wuz layin' on the hospittul bunk with his dead side kivered over with a pris'n blankit, an' his wife a-cryin' becase the ward'n war 'bleeged ter lock her out, the Gov'ner his se'f walked in. An' what yer reckin he done? Cried! What yer think o' that, cully? Cried; an' lowed ez how 'few folks wuz so bad et somebody didn't keer fur 'em,' an' then he called the man's wife back, an' p'inted ter the half dead ole convic', an' told her ter 'fetch him home.' Did! An' the nex' day if the Banner didn't tan him! Yer jest bet it did.

22

"An' ther' wuz a feller ther' been in twenty year, an' had seventy-nine more ahead uv him. An' one night when ther' wa'n't nobody thinkin' uv it, he up an' got erligion. An' he ain't no more en got it, en he wants ter git away fum ther'. Prayed fur it constant: 'Lord, let me out!' 'Lord, let me out!' That's what he ud say ez he set on the spoke pile fittin' spokes fur the Tennessee wagins; an' a-cryin' all the time. He couldn't take time ter cry an' pray 'thout cheat'n' o' the State, yer know, so he jest cried an' prayed while he worked. The other pris'ners poked fun at him; an' tol' him if he got out they ud try erligion in theirn. Yorter seen him; he wuz a good un. Spec' yer have heerd about him. Did yer heear 'bout the big fire that bruk out in the pris'n las' November, did yer?"

The Governor nodded and the boy talked on.

"Well, that ther' convic' worked orful hard at that fire. He fetched thirteen men out on his back. They wuz suf'cated, yer know. He fetched the warden out, too, in his arms. An' one uv his arms wuz burnt that bad it had ter be cut off. An' the pris'n doctor said he breathed fire inter his lungs or somethin'. An' the next day the Gov'ner pard'ned uv him out. I wuz ther' when the pard'n come. The warden's voice trim'led when he read it ter the feller layin' bundled up on his iron bunk. An' when he heeard it he riz up in bed an' sez he, 'My prayers is answered, tell the boys.' The warden bent over 'im ez he dropped back an' shet his eyes, an' tried ter shake him up. 'What must I tell the Gov'ner?' sez he. 'Tell him, God bless him.' An' that wuz the las' word he ever did say topside o' this earth. Whatcher think o' that, cully? 'Bout ez big ez the Banner's growl, wa'n't it?"

The Executive nodded again, while the little gossip of the slums talked on in his quaint, old way, of deeds the very

23

angels must have wept to witness, so full were they of glorious humanity.

"But the best uv all wuz about ole Bemis," said he, re-arranging his tatters so that the undried portion might be turned to the fire. "Did you ever heear about ole Bemis?"

Did he? Would he ever cease to hear about him, he wondered. Was there, could there be any excuse for him there? The evening Independent thought not. Yet he felt some curiosity to know how his "chicken-hearted foolishness" had been received in the slums, so he motioned the boy to go on. Verily the tattered gossip had never had so rapt a listener.

"Yer see," said he, "Bemis wuz a banker; a reg'lar rich un. He kilt a man,--kilt him dead, too,--an' yer see, cully, 'twas his own son-in-law. An' one cote went dead against him, an' they fetched it ter t'other, 's'preme' or 'sperm,' or somethin'. An' the Banner said 'he orter be hung, an' would be if the Guv'ner'd let him. But if he'd cry a little the Guv'ner'd set him on his feet again, when the cotes wuz done with him.' But that cote said he mus' hang, too, an' they put him in jail; an' befo' they had the trial, the jailer looked fur a mob ter come an' take him out at night an' hang him. He set up late lookin' fur it. But stid uv a mob, the jailer heerd a little pitapat on the steps, an' a little rattle uv the door, an' when he opened uv it ther' wuz a little lame cripple girl standin' ther' leanin' on her crutches a-cryin', an' a-beggin' ter see her pappy. Truth, cully; cross my heart" (and two small fingers drew the sign of the cross upon the little gossip's breast). "Atter that, folks begin ter feel sorry fur the ole banker, when the jailer 'd tell about the little crutch ez sounded up'n down them jail halls all day. The pris'ners got ter know it, an' ter wait fur it, an' they named uv her 'crippled angul,' she wuz that white an' pritty, with her blue eyes, an' hair like tumbled-up sunshine all round her face. When the pris'ners heerd the restle uv her little silk dress breshin' the banisters ez she clomb upstairs, they ud say, 'Ther's the little angul's wings.' An' they said the jail got more darker after the wings went by. An' when they had that ther' las' trial uv ole Bemis, lots o' meanness leaked out ez had been done him, an' it showed ez the pris'ner wa'n't so mightily ter blame atter all. An' lots of folks wuz hopin' the ole man ud be plumb cleared. But the cote said he mus' hang, hang, hang. Did; an' when it said so the angul fell over in her pappy's arms, an' her crutch rolled down an' lay aginst the judge's foot, an' he picked it up an' heft it in his hen' all the time he wuz saying o' the death sentence.

"An' the Banner said 'that wuz enough fur chicken-heart,'--an' said ever'body might look fur a pard'n nex' day. An' then whatcher reckin? What do yer reckin, cully? The nex' day down come a little yeller-headed gal ter the jail a-kerryin uv a pard'n. Whatcher think o' that? Wuz that chicken heart? Naw, cully, that wuz grit. Skinny said so. An' Skinny said,--he wuz allus hangin' roun' the cap'tul,--an' he heerd the men talkin' 'bout it. An' they said the little gal come up ter see the Gov'ner, an' he wouldn't see her at first. But she got in at last, an' begged an' begged fur the ole man 'bout ter hang.

"But the Gov'ner wouldn't lis'n, till all's once she turned ter him an' sez she, 'Have you got a chile?' An' his eyes filt up in a minute, an' sez he, 'One, at Mount Olivet.' That's the graveyard, yer know. Then he called his sec't'ry man, an' whispered ter him. An' the man sez, 'Is it wise?' An' then the Gov'ner stood up gran' like, an' sez he, 'Hit's right; an' that's enough.' Wa'n't that bully, though? Wa'n't it? Say, cully, whatcher think o' that? An' whatcher lookin' at out the winder?"

The shadows held the tall warrior in a dusky mantle. Was it fancy, or did old Hickory indeed lift his cocked hat a trifle higher? Old bronze hero, did he, too, hear that click of a child's crutch echoing down the dismal corridors of the grim old State House, as the little, misshapen feet sped upon their last hope? And in his dreams did he too hear, the Executive wondered, the cry of a little child begging life of him who alone held it? Did he hear the wind, those long December nights, moaning over Olivet with the sob of a dead babe in its breath? Did he understand the human, as well as the heroic, old warrior-statesman whose immortality, was writ in bronze?

"Say, cully," the tatters grew restless again, "does the firelight hurt yer eyes, makes 'em water? They looks like the picture o' Skinny's man when the water's in 'em so. Oh, but hit's a good picture. It's a man, layin' in bed. Sick or somethin', I reckin.' An' his piller's all ruffled up, an' the kiverlid all white ez snow. An' his face has got a kind o' glory look, jest like yer see on the face o' the pris'n chaplin when he's a-prayin' with his head up, an' his eyes shet tight, an' a streak o' sunshine comes a-creepin' in through the gratin' uv the winders an' strikes acrost his face. That's the way Skinny's picture man looks, only ther' ain't no bars, an' the light stays ther'. An' in one corner is a big, big patch o' light. 'Tain't sunshine, too soft. An' 'tain't moonlight, too bright. Hit's dest light. An' plumb square in the middle uv it is a angul: a gal angul, I reckin, becase its orful pretty, with goldish hair, an' eyes ez blue ez--that cheer yer head's leaned on. An' she has a book, a gold un; whatcher think o' that? An she's writin' down names in it. An' the man in the bed is watchin' uv her, an' tellin' uv her what ter do; for down ter the bottom ther's some gol'-writin'. Skinny figgered it out an' it said, 'Write me as one who loves his fellow men.' Ain't that scrumptious? Yer jest bet.

"I asked Skinny once what it meant, and he said he didn't know fur plumb certain' but sez he, 'I calls it the Gov'ner, Skip: the Gov'ner an' the crippled angul.' Atter that Skinny an' me an' the boys allus called it the Gov'ner. Say! did you ever see the Gov'ner?"

The Executive nodded; and the tatters rising and sinking back again with vehemence in accord with surprise, threatened to leave more than a single mark upon the State's purple.

"Oh, say now! did yer though? An' did he look this here way, an' set his chin so, an' keep his eyes kind o' shet 's if he wuz afeard someun ud see if he cried an' tell the Banner ez ther' wuz tears in his eyes? Skinny said he did. Skinny didn't lie, he didn't.

"An' did yer ever heear him make a speech? Raily now, did yer?"

The spare body bent forward, as if the sharp eyes would catch the faintest hint of falsehood in the face before him. "Yorter heerd him. Skinny did once, when he wuz 'norgrated, yer know. An' you bet he's gran', then, on them 'norgrat'n days. He jest up an' dares the ole Banner. An' his speeches goes this er way."

The tatters half stood; the sole of one torn shoe pressed against the State's purple of the great easy-chair, one resting upon the velvet rug. One small hand lightly clasped the arm of the cherry chair, while the other was enthusiastically waved to and fro as the vagabond's deft tongue told off a fragment of one of the Executive's masterpieces of eloquence and oratory.

27

"Out of the mouths of babes and sucklings," indeed, poured the great particle of the great argument that had swept the old Volunteer State, at the moment of its financial agony, from center to circumference:

" 'The so-called "State Bonds" are against the letter and spirit of the Constitution of the United States, which declares, No State shall grant letters of marque and reprisal, coin money, or emit bills of credit. State bonds! State bonds! I tell you, friends and fellow-citizens, that is the name of the enemy that is hammering upon that mighty platform upon which all social, political, and financial affairs of the country are founded; the palladium of our liberties,--the Constitution of the United States.' "

The ragged shoe slipped from its velvet pedestal, the now dry tatters dropped back into the luxuriant softness of the easy-chair. The glow of excitement faded from the little old face that seemed suddenly to grow older. The man watching with keen surprise, that was indeed almost wonder, saw the boy's thin lips twitch nervously. The great speech was forgotten in the mighty memories it had stirred. The tattered sleeve was drawn across the face that was tattered too, and it was full two minutes by the State's bronze clock, before the vagabond held control of his feelings.

"Say!" he ventured again, "yorter knowed Skinny. He wuz the nicest boy yevver did see. He knowed ever'thing, he did. See the Gov'ner many a time. Heerd him say that very speech I'm tellin' you about. In this very house, too, upstairs, wher' the leguslater sets. I peeped in while ago; nobody ther' but the sextent. Skinny heerd the Gov'ner speak ther' though--an' when the ban' played, an' the folks all clapped their hands, Skinny flung his hat up, plumb inter the big chand'ler, an' hollered out: 'Hooray for the Gov'ner an' the Low Taxers!' an' a p'liceman fetched him out by the collar, an' when he got out the cop sez ter him, sez he, 'Now whatcher got ter say?' Skinny wuz a Low Taxer his own se'f, so when the cop axed him for his say, he flung his hat up todes the bare-headed Liberty woman out ther' at the front door, an' sez he, 'Hooray! fur the Gov'ner an' the Low Tax party.' Did. He slep' in the lock-up that night fur it, you bet; but he got his holler. He wuz a plumb good un.

"Say, cully! I wisht yer could see Skinny's picture anyhow. It's over ter hunchback Harry's house now, t'other side o' Hell's Half. Yer know Hell's Half acre? Awful place. Skinny give the picture ter Harry 'count o' his not bein' able ter git about much. He set a sight o' store by it, Skinny did, an' he didn't let it leave him till the las' minit; he just willed it, yer know, to hunchback Harry. When he wuz a-dyin' he turned ter me, an' sez he, 'Skip, hang the Gov'ner so's I can see him.' An' when I done it, he sez, sorter smilin', sez he, 'Skip?' Sez I, 'Skinny!' Sez he, 'The crippled angul has wiped all the tears out o' the Gov'ner's eyes.' Then he fell back on his straw piller an' shet his eyes, so; an' after while he opened uv um, an' sez he--so soft yer jest could a-heerd it; sez he, 'Write me ez one who loves his fellow-men.' An' that wuz the las' word he ever said on this earth. He had a nice fun'ril; yer bet. Us newsboys made it; an' the pris'n chaplain said the sument. We bought the flowers, us boys , they cos' ten dollars. Ther' wuz a wreath made uv white roses, an' right in the middle, made out o' little teeny buds, wuz his name--'Skinny.' The flower-man said it wouldn't do, when we told him ter put it ther,' but we 'lowed 'twuz our money and our fun'ril and if we couldn't have it our way we wouldn't have it at all. An' he said it might hurt his folkses' feelin's; but we tol' him Skinny didn't have no folks, an' no name neither, 'cept jest 'Skinny.' So he made up the wreath like we said, an' it's out ther' on his grave this blessed minit, if the snow ain't kivered it up. Say, cully!

Don't yer be a-cryin' fur Skinny. He's all right-- the chaplain sez so. The Gov'ner'd cry fur him though, I bet yer, if he knowed about the fun'ril yistiddy. Mebbe ole Pop-Hick'ry wouldn't, but I bet the Gov'ner would."

The face of the Executive was turned toward the fire-- a tiny, blue blaze shot upward for an instant, and was reflected in a diamond setting that glittered upon his bosom. A match to the sparkling jewel rested a moment upon his cheek, then rolled down and lay upon his hand--a bright, glistening tear. There was a sound of heavy footsteps coming down the gray stone corridor--a creak, a groan, and a bang.

"What's that?" asked the newsboy, starting up.

"That," said the Executive, "is the porter, closing up for the night."

The tatters stood as near upright as tatters may, and gathered themselves together. Not a paper sold; he had gossiped away the afternoon with right royal recklessness. He remembered it too late.

"Say! yer wouldn't want a Herald?" It was not easy to talk business where lately he had talked confidence. The Executive's hand sought his pocket.

"Yes," said he, "a Herald will do. What is your name, boy?"

"Skippy! 'cause I don't skip, yer know."

There was a twinkle in the vagabond's eye, as the maimed foot was thrust forward. The next moment he glanced at the coin the Executive had handed him.

"Say! I can't change a dollar; hadn't seen that much money since the bridge wuz burnt."

The Executive smiled. "Never mind the change," said he, "and be sure you bring me to-morrow's Herald."

The tatters did stand upright at that, while a look of genuine wonder, not unmixed with admiration, came into the little old-young face.

"Say! who be you anyhow?" he asked. And the lids did "drop," as the Banner said "to hide the tears," as the great man answered slowly:--

"I am the Governor of Tennessee, Skip."

There was a low soft whistle, a hurried shambling toward the door, a half-whispered something about "Skinny" and "old Pop-Hickory," and the ponderous door closed behind him. When the fire had burned so low he could no longer see the print of the newsboy's foot upon the velvet cushion of the arm-chair, the Governor arose and began to put away his papers.

"Inasmuch as she was sorely wronged" --his eye fell upon a line of the woman-murderer's long petition. Was this a "case for clemency," as the petition declared? The crisp paper rattled strangely as he unrolled it, and fixed his own name, together with the great seal of the State, to the few words he had written. It is a grand thing to hold life in the hand: a thing next to God himself. It is a grander thing to give life, and nearer to God, too, for is not God the giver of all life? The long petition lay in the Executive's private drawer; his day's work was done; to-morrow the despised afternoon journal would sum it up so: "Pardoned another red-handed Cain." The angels perhaps might record it

31

something after this wise: "Saved another soul from hell."
He sighed, and thrust the few remaining papers into the
drawer, locked it, and made ready to go home. For the
darkness had indeed fallen; the bronze statue, as he sought
it through the window, had become only a part of the
bronze night. But the heart of old Hickory was there, in his
own bosom, throbbing and alive with the burden of
humanity. To-morrow the critics might lash; but to-night--
he opened the door of the great gray corridor; the wind
swept with a sepulchral groan through the vault- like
gloom; he lifted his face to the leaden sky, starless and
cold.--"Write me," he said, "as one who loves his fellow-
men;" and blushed, as any hero might, to find his heart as
brave as its convictions.

FIDDLING HIS WAY TO FAME.

WE had fallen in with a party of Alabama boys, and all having the same end in view, --a good time--we joined forces and pitched our tents on the bank of the Clinch, the prettiest stream in Tennessee, and set about enjoying ourselves after our own approved fashion.

Even the important-looking gentleman, sitting over against a crag where he had dozed and smoked for a full hour, forgot, for the nonce, that he was other than wit and wag for the company; the jolly good fellow he, the free man (once more), and the huntsman.

Our division had followed the hounds since sun-up; the remainder of the company were still out upon the river with rod and line. The sun was about ready to drop behind Lone Mountain, that solitary peak, of nobody knows precisely what, that keeps a kind of solemn guard upon the wayward little current singing at its base. Supper was ready; the odor of coffee, mingled with a no less agreeable aroma of broiling bacon, and corn cake, was deliciously tantalizing to a set of weary hunters. But we were to wait for the boys, that was one of our rules, always observed. The sun set, and twilight came on with that subtle light that is half gloom, half glow, and mingled, or tried to, with the red glare of the camp-fire.

While we sat there, dozing and waiting, there was a break in the brush below the bluff upon which we were camped. "A deer!" One of the boys reached for his rifle, just as a tall, gaunt figure appeared above the bluff, catching as he came at the sassafras and hazel bushes, pulling himself up until he stood among us a very Saul in height, and a Goliath, to all seeming, in strength.

He took in the camp, the fire, and the group at a glance. But the figure over against the crag caught his best attention There was a kind of telegraphic recognition of some description, for the giant smiled and nodded.

"Howdye," he said; and our jolly comrade took his pipe from between his lips and returned the salutation in precisely the same tone in which it was given.

"Howdye; be you-uns a-travelin'?"

The giant nodded, and passed on, and our comrade dropped back against the crag, and returned to his pipe. But a smile played about his lips, as if some very tender recollection had been stirred by the passing of the gaunt stranger.

It was one of the Alabama boys who broke the silence that had fallen upon us. He had observed the sympathetic recognition that passed between the two men, and had noted the naturalness with which the "dialect" had been returned.

"I'll wager my portion of the supper," he said, "that he is a Tennessean, and from the hill country." He pointed in the direction taken by the stranger. He missed, however, the warning--"Sh!" from the Tennessee side.

"A Tennessee mountaineer--" he went on. "His speech bewrayeth him."

Then one of our boys spoke right out.

"Look out!" said he, "the Governor is from the hill country too."

The silence was embarrassing, until the man over against the crag took the pipe from between his lips, and struck the bowl upon his palm gently, the smile still lingering about his mouth.

"Yes," he said, "I was born among the hills of Tennessee. 'The Barrens,' geologists call it; the poets name it 'Land of the Sky.' My heart can find for it no holier name than--home."

The Governor leaned back against the crag. We knew the man, and wondered as to the humor that was upon him. Politician, wit, comrade, gentleman; as each we knew him. But as native, mountaineer, ah! he was a stranger to us in that rôle. We had heard of the quaint ease with which he could drop into the speech of his native hills, no less than the grace with which he filled the gubernatorial chair.

He had "stumped the state" twice as candidate, once as elector. His strange, half-humorous, half-pathetic oratory was familiar in every county from the mountains to the Mississippi. But the native;--we almost held our breath while the transformation took place, and the governor-orator for the moment became the mountaineer.

"I war born," he said, "on the banks o' the Wataugy, in the county uv Cartir,--in a cabin whose winders opened ter the East, an' to'des the sunrise. That war my old mother's notion an' bekase it war her notion it war allus right ter me. Fur she was not one given ter wrong ideas.

"I war her favorite chil' uv the seven God give. My cheer set nighest hers. The yeller yarn that slipped her shiny needles first slipped from hank ter ball across my sunburnt wrists. The mug uv goldish cream war allus at my plate; the cl'arest bit uv honey-comb, laid cross the biggis' plug uv pies war allus set fur me. The bit o' extry sweetnin' never missed my ole blue chiny cup.

"An' summer days when fiel' work war a-foot, a bottle full o' fraish new buttermilk war allus tucked away amongst the corn pones in my dinner pail.

"An' when I tuk ter books, an' readin' uv the papers, an' the ole man riz up ag'inst it, bekase I war more favored ter the book nor ter the plough then my old mount'n mammy, ez allus stood 'twixt me an' wrath, she riz up too, an' bargained with the ole man fur two hours uv my time. This war the bargain struck. From twelve er'clock ontil the sun marked two upon the kitchen doorstep I war free.

"Ever' day fur this much I war free. An' in my stid, whilst I lay under the hoss apple tree an' figgered out my book stuff, she followed that ole plough up an' down the en'less furrers across that hot ontrodd'n fiel'--in my stid.

"I've travelled some sence then, ploughed many a furrer in the fiel' o' this worl's troubles, an' I hev foun' ez ther' be few ez keers tur tek the plough whilst I lay by ter rest.

"An' when the work war done, an' harvest in, I tuk ter runnin' down o' nights ter hear the boys discuss the questions o' the day at Jube Turner's store over ter the settlemint.

" 'Twar then the ole man sot his foot down.

" 'It hev ter stop!' he said. 'The boy air comin' ter no good.'

"Then my ole mammy riz agin, an' set down ez detarmint ez him; an' sez she:--

" 'He be a man, an' hev the hankerin's uv a man. The time hev come fur me ter speak. The boy must hev his l'arnin'-books his min' calls fur. He aims ter mix with men; an' you an' me, ole man, must stand aside, an' fit him fur the wrestle ez be boun' ter come. Hit air bespoke fur him, an' ther' ben't no sense in henderin' sech ez be bespoke beforehan'.'

"She kerried, an' I went ter school. The house air standin' now--a cabin in the valley, nigh the banks o' the Wataugy. I tuk ter books, they said, like beans ter cornstalks. An' winter nights I'd pile the pine knots on the fire, to light me ter the secrets uv them blue an' yeller kivers.

"An' she'd set by an' holp me with her presence, my ole mount'n mother would. She even holped to gether up the pine knots when the days war over short. She holped me ever way. Her heart retched down ter mine an' l'arned its needs, an' holped ter satisfy them. She flung the rocks out uv my way, openin' up the path before--the path her partial eye had sighted, every inch uv it.

"She saved the butter an' sent it off ter the settlemint ter sell it, so's I could hev a daily paper, when she see ez I war hankerin' fur it.

"An' when it kem, I'd set ther' on a kaig an' read it ter the mount'n boys, an' Jube; they-uns flocked ter me like crows flockin' ter a corn-field; an' me it war, a mount'n stripplin', ez dealt the word o' politics ter they-uns.

"But somthin' worrit me: a hitch war in my l'arnin'. Still, the ole man in the cabin begin ter grow more easy-like an' teok ter readin' an' war not ill-pleased ter git the news. An' he fretted sometimes ef I tarried ter the store, bekase he war a-waitin' fur the news. But I war troubled; and that eye ez war allus open ter my ailments see that I war worrit. An' one day when I kem down the road, she met me, my ole mammy, an' she put her hand onter my arm, an' walked along o' me. An' sez she:--

" 'What air it, son, ez be a-troublin' uv ye, I be yer mammy, an' ez sech yer frien', an' I aims ter know yer ailments.'

"An' I tuk that tremblin' hand close inter mine, an' I spoke my min', my feelin's, freely.

" 'I be worrit,' sez I, 'becase I be onable ter make out ef I be right or no.'

" 'In politics?' sez she.

" 'Yaas,' sez I, 'in politics. I git but one side o' the matter, an' I know ez ther' be two. An' I ben't satisfied with this side, an' still I be onable ter make out the other!'

"She onriddled me at onc't.

" 'You-uns must hev the other paper, son,' sez she. 'Your granddad war a politician under Clay; en' ther' war two sides then, an' ther' air boun' ter be two now, although the word uv it may not retch the Wataugy.'

"I never will furgit the first day it kem, that Dimercratic paper. I went ter the settlemint, I knowed the paper war a comin, an' I guessed what it would be; a coal o' fire ter that Republican stronghold.

"I tuk my fiddle down; it war my mother's thought.

" 'Play 'em Sally Gal,' sez she, 'afore the mail comes.'

"I done it; an' they-uns war toler'ble frien'ly; fur the mount'n boys allus hev a weakness fur a fiddle an' a mount'n fiddler.

"But when the mail war opened--Laud! how they swore an' tuk on. Some laffed; a mighty few though, an' some winked ter one ernother. Some cussed outright an' all war thunderstruck. Ez fur me, I went out ter it, an' it kem in ter me. I war a Dimercrat from that good day.

"I tuk it home; the ole man list'ned, countin' it a mighty joke ter hear me an' brother Alf argerfyin' 'bout the two sides, an' sometimes he'd say which beat in argerfyin', but he mostly allus went with Alf. Bimeby Alf tuk the Republican paper, ez my time give out, an' we-uns went tergether ter the settlemint; an' we'd mount a kaig, him on one, and me on t'other, and we'd give the news ter both sides, him an' me. Some few sided long o' me, but most war tuk to Alf. An' so it war understood ez I war Dimercrat, and Alf Republican.

"It tickled the ole man mightily. He useter call in the Wataugy boys ter hear us argerfy o' nights, and they-uns sot in jedgmint ez ter which uv we-uns war the best at sech. Alf allus got the vote, an' one night I riz up; fur I war mad some, an' I give the word ez how a Dimercrat would never stan' no chance o' justice in sech a onfair destrict. They-uns laffed, but ther was one ez sot her face aginst sech. 'A house set against itself air boun' ter come ter bad luck,' my ole mother said.

"One day ther' war a meetin' ter the settlemint, a political meetin', an' Jube war buckin' up the boys right pears, an' war about ter sweep off everthing. I moved about a bit among they-uns, an' after a little the word war giv ez ther' war a split.

"Then kem a row, an' Jube he druv the Dimercrats out 'n o' his store, an' they held the'r meetin' in the blacksmith's shop. An' I war goin' out along o' they-uns, an' Jube see me; an' he sez, sez he:--

" 'Come back here, Bob, an' vote your good ole daddy's principles.' Fur Jube war boss o' that ther' destrict. But I war mad, an' I sez, sez I:--

" 'I aims ter vote my own principles,' sez I, 'an' they be Dimercratic.'

"An' when that day war over, ole Si Ridley he rid over ter we-uns' cabin on the Wataugy an' give the word as I war nominated ter the Legislatur aginst big Judge Griggsby, the rankest Republican ter all that county.

"Then the ole man riz up in real dead earnest. He named me fur a idiot an' a upstart, an' let on ez how he never 'lowed that playful argerfyin' o' Alf an' me would ever be tuk fur more'n a little playful talk.

"He swore he'd thrash the heresy out o' me. Then my ole mammy, she riz up.

" 'Nary lick, Josiah,' sez she. 'He hev the right ter choose, an' he hev done it.'

"Then he give the word ez he'd vote aginst me same's he would any other Dimercrat. He kept his word. On the day uv election him an' the boys went over ter Jube's ter vote.

"Folks showed considerable interest, allowing ez blood war more stronger nor politics, an' that the ole man would come over ter me in the eend.

"But he didn't; he jest voted clean an' open fur Griggsby, an' I 'lowed the boys would foller his lead. But when my oldest brother stepped up an' drapped in a vote fur me, I cl'ar furgot myself, an' I jest flung up my hat an' shouted, 'Count one fur the Dimercrat.'

"The ole man war pow'ful mad. But when Alf an' Dave an' Hugh voted with him, it kinder eased him some. But when the next cast lots with me, I yelled again.

" 'Hooray fur Dimocracy!' sez I. An' the ole man he jest lifted up his ridin' switch, an' sez he:--

" 'Stop, sir! Take off your coat, sir. I'll thrash that Dimocracy out o' you.'

"Ye could a heerd a pin drap. Then I ketched ole Jube Turner's eye. He allus 'lowed ther' war no backbone to a Dimercrat. An' when I see him I flung back my coat an' bowed my shoulders fur the ole man's lash.

"The boys drapped back, disappointed, an' I heard a hiss ez the first blow fell. Forty licks. I tuk 'em without a tremble. An' when the last un fell, I riz up an' tore off my hat, an' tossed it up ter the rafters, an' sez I, ez loud ez I could, 'Hooray fur Dimocracy! Forty lashes hev heat it ter redhot heat.'

"Then a yell went up, an' I knowed ez Carter County war gone Dimercratic fur onc't, afore ole Jube stepped out afore the boys, an' tuk off his hat an' sez, 'I be fur the feller ez can't be beat out o' his principles.'

"Them war stormy times in the cabin on the Wataugy, I kin tell ye. The boys built a bonfire top o' Lynn Mount'n jest acrost the river. It lit up the kentry fur miles, an' my ole mammy watched it through her tears ez she stood in the cabin door; but the old man didn't speak ter me no more till I war startin' off ter Nashvill ter tek my seat, ez 'the member from Carter.'

"But my ole mammy follered me down ter the settlement, wher' the boys war waitin' ter say good-by, an' she tuk my hen' 'n hers, an' sez she:--

" 'Legislatur or plow-boy, remember ye air born to die!'

" 'Mend up the road law,' said Jube, at partin', 'an' let down the gap ter the still house.' Fur Jube had a taste fur apple-juice an' corn squeezin's.

"Waal, I moved along toler'ble pears. Ef I could set the boys a-laffin', I war toler'ble sartin' ter kerry my p'int. Ef I couldn't, someun would move adjournmint, 'Ter give Bob time ter ile up,' they said. 'Ilin' up ' meant gettin' my fiddle ready an' callin' the boys tergether in a committee room or somewher's, an' tollin' 'em inter measures with 'Rabbit in the Pea Patch'--'Chicken in the Bread Tray'--an' some o' the other mount'n tunes. The mount'n boys war allus sure to come under after a pull at the ole fiddle. It jest put 'em inter a kind o' jubilee that would a' let the State o' Tennessee go ter the devul, ef unly the fiddle war left.

" 'Remember ye air born ter die.' I could hear it in the twang o' the fiddlestrings, a-playin' the boys inter harness, in the clerk's voice a-callin' the roll, in the speaker's gavil a-knockin' fur order.

"One mornin' ther' war a big railroad bill afore the House, an' the Dimercrats went one side the track, and the Republicans went t'other. An' I sot ther' awaitin' my turn ter vote; an' when it kem, I riz up scarcely knowin' what I war a-doin', an' sez I:--

" 'I be born ter die! I be aginst that bill.'

"An' the boys set up a yell, a-callin' ter me not ter do it. An' the nex' day the papers named me fur a Jonah, an' said ez I war showin' uv the East Tennessee streak ter my bacon. The streak in East Tennessee bacon air a Republican streak, they 'lowed. An' they made game o' my sayin' I war born ter die. I went ter bed that night toler'ble crushed. But in my dreams, I war back ter the fair valley o' the Wataugy, en' a face deep- scarred an' wrinkled riz up afore me, an a pair o' faded eyes looked inter mine, an' I heeard the voice o' my ole mammy, 'Stan' by your principles. Ye air born to die!'

"So I went 'long. One day ther' war a mighty rumpus over a bill to shet off gamblin' in the State o' Tennessee. Times were hot, an' word war give ez how some aimed ter hev that bill, spite o' locks an' safes an' clerks an' sergeants. Ther' war a night session. An' I war at it. An' ez I run my hen' inter my desk, it fetched a package. I tuk it up; pinned ter it war a note. '$5,000 fur a vote against the Gamblin' Bill,' it said. I dropped my head on my desk an' groaned. I war unly a mount'n stripplin', an' that temptation war orful, orful.

" 'Remember ye air born ter die.' Ole mount'n mother. I could hear her voice above the voice o' the tempter.

"When my name war called, I riz up, that roll o' gunpowder in my hand. I heft it out afore 'em all, high up ez I could retch, en' I yelled out in reg'lar mount'n fashion-- 'Who bids ?' sez I, 'who bids? Five thousan' fur some man's honor. Come an' git it whosoever air minded. Ez fur me, I air not a bidder.'

"An' I flung it with all my might acrost the house, an' I heeard it fall at the clerk's feet ez I called ter him to put me down fur that bill. 'Fur it, till the crack o' doom.'

"Laud! I never kalkulated on raisin' such a rumpus. I war the bigges' man in Tennessee that night. I went ter bed, ter be woke up by the brass band under my winder, a-playin' 'Hail ter the Chief.'

"I war allus a fool about a band anyhow, an' when I heeard that grand old tune, played fur me,--me, I jest drapped back 'mongst the kivers and cried like a baby.

"Me, hid away in a forty-ninth class bo'rdin' house,--me, the plow-boy o' the Wataugy. Then the boys bust in an' ordered me inter my clothes, an' drug me out fur a speech. An' when I heeard the yellin', sez I, 'Boys, in the name o' creation what hev I done?' An' some-un said, sez he, 'Ye've turned the water-pipe loose on hell,--that's what ye've done.'

"I went home shortly after that--went a-wonderin' what Jube would say. Fur Jube war toler'ble fond uv ole Sledge now'n then.

"Waal, I hev hed some success, I say it meekly; an' I hev felt some little pride, I say it meekly; an' I hev hed some happy minutes in my life. But the happies' minute I ever knowed war that minute when I sot my foot on my native East Tennessee sile agin, an' felt the hand o' honest old Jube Turner tek holt o' mine an' wring it hard whilst he looked away to'des the blue hills for the tears war in his eyes, an' sez he 'Ye'll do ter trust, youngster!'

"The ox-wagin war ther' ter meet me ter fetch me up the mount'n. The ole steers Buck and Bill, hed flags a-flyin' from ther horns, an' the wagin war all kivered up in cedar branches an' the pretty pink azalea that growed right around our cabin door An' h'isted squar' on top uv all war a pole a sign-board, with a flag a-flyin', an' on it m' ole school-marm hed writ a line:--

" 'The plow-boy o' the Wataugy; Truth, the sledge hammer o' the mountaineer !'

"An' how the boys did shout! They fairly drug me ter the wagin, an' then all fell inter line, an' sot out fur the cabin long side the Wataugy.

"Home! that little cabin wher' the winders turned ter meet the sun; the waters sing ther' all the year aroun', sing and sob. One part the pretty river red'nin' in the sun, an' t'other dead black with the shadow uv the pines that cap the summit uv Lynn Mount'n.

"An' the boys come down ter meet me at the bars, an' the ole man, proud uv his son, ashamed uv the Dimercrat, leanin' on his staff under the greenin' hop-vines. An', best uv all, the vision uv a little woman standin' in the door, shadin' her eyes aginst the sunlight, waitin' fur her boy.

"The flag floated above my head; the boys yelled the'rse'ves hoarse; the wagin creaked, an' Jube's whip cracked about the spotted steer's back. But I heeard nothin'; I seed nothin', but my mother waitin' in the door. She tuk me in her arms, an' drapped her cheek upon my bosom.

" 'My boy,' she said; an' it war wuth ten times over the whole that I hed won.

"But the ole man war worrit. A sign pinned ter the wagin-hed hed tuk his eye.

" 'The Champion o' Democracy' it said.

" 'Take it down,' said some one, 'it worries the ole man." An' one riz up ter cut it down. But I war ther' afore him, an' I retched out ter take the hand that would cut away my colors.

" 'Stop!' sez I. 'Boys,' I went on, 'they be my colors. I'll not hide 'em from the eye uv God or man.'

"Then they raised a shout: 'Them colors'll stan' ye good stead fur Congress,' they said, 'bimeby.'

"They done it. It war this way. Ther' war foul play in the convention, the Republican convention. An' ole Bony Pettibrash, who aimed to boss that kentry, got the nomination. That riled the boys, and they-uns swore he never should be elected. So when the Dimercrats nomernated me, the t'other elemint being ag'inst ole Pettibrash come out fur me, an' I went ter Congress.

"I had ter work fur it though, fur Pettibrash hed his follerin'. He war a pow'ful hand at argerfyin', though not much on a joke. He war long-winded, an' my unly chance war in the fac' that the boys got tired uv him. I laid my plans--'twas my ole mammy holped me, an' suggested.

"One night we-uns war ter meet at the log schoolhouse an' discuss matters. A big crowd war ter be ther', an' I tuk my fiddle along, accerdentally, so ter speak. The boys war lookin' oneasy.

" 'Can't ye tell a good coon yarn, Bob?' they sez. But Jube 'lowed a 'possum story ez I knowed would tek better.

"Then I whispered in Jube's ear the plan I hed laid out.

"Jest afore speakin' time I onwropped my fiddle an' twanged a string.

" 'Give us a tune, Bob,' sung out Jube 'ter liven us up a bit whilst we're waitin'.'

"I tetched the bow across the strings. 'Rabbit in the Pea-Patch,'--the boys began ter pat; soft at first, then a bit more pears. Then I played up--that ole Rabbit went a-skippin' an' a-trippin', I kin tell ye. Far' well ter the peas in that patch. How the boots did strike that ole puncheon floor! Jube led. I could hear his leather 'bove all the rest.

"All 't onc't I struck inter 'Rollin' River'; fur I see ole Pettibrash eyein' uv me through the winder. Jube see it, too--an' sez he--'Plenty o' time, boys, fur speakin'. Out with the benches, an' let's hev a dance.'--Out they went, an' the gals an' wimmen folks kem in; an' then I tuk the teacher's desk, an' put my fiddle ter my shoulder, an' sez I, 'Boys, ef ye'd rether hev cat-gut music ez ter hev chin, I'm yer man. But I'll jest mek all the speech I've got ter mek in mighty few words. It air this: I'm agin the Blair Bill an' fur the fair thing. Them's my sentiments in Congress or on the mount'n.'

"Then I fetched up the fiddle, an' give 'em 'Chicken in the Bread Tray,' whilst ole Pettibrash war left ter chew the ragged eend o' disapp'intment. It war midnight when we quit. We offered ter 'divide time' about eleven o'clock, but the boys war in fur a frolic. Waal, we-uns went to Congress, me an' the fiddle. An' that ole fiddle went long o' me ter all the speakin's afore it went ter Congress, an' it beat ole Pettibrash all ter hollow fur argumint. 'Fiddled his way ter Congress,' the papers said, an' they didn't miss it ez fur ez I hev knowed 'em ter do.

"But the fiddle war not done yit. The papers talked mightily about it, an' about me 'fiddlin' my way ter fame' an' sech.

"One day a question kem up fur the protection uv iron, an' I voted fur it, long with the Republicans. Ye see I war a mount'n boy; an' them ole hills o' Tennessee, sech ez war not filled with marble, war chuck full o' iron or coal, or sech. I war boun' ter stan' by the mount'n. The papers abused me mightily, an' 'lowed ez I played the wrong tune that time.

"That night I had a diff'rint surrenade, on mighty diff'rint instrumints from the ole Tennessee brass band. They war tin horns, an' busted buckets, an' cowbells; an' ther' war a feller ez give out the tunes, an' one war this:--

" 'The Whelp o' the Wataugy,' an' the band applauded right along.

"The next war:--

" 'The Fiddlin' Mugwump,' an' the band seconded the motion.

" 'The Protection 'Possum o' the Cumberlands' fetched down the house.

"Then some-un called fur me, an' I went out, me an' the fiddle. An' I didn't say a word; I jist fetched the bow across the strings, an' begin ter play,--

'Kerry me back,
Kerry me back ter Tennessee!'

"Fur a minute all war still ez the dead. Then some-un shouted, 'Go it, Bob!' An' the whole earth fairly shuk with the'r shoutin'.

" 'Fiddle away, ole coon,' they hollered. "Go it, my whelp!'--'Hooray fur Tennessee!'

"The next mornin' ther' war a big poplar coffin settin' on the steps o' my bo'din' house an' a big fiddle laid 'pon top o' it, an' on a white card war painted in blackletters: 'Hang up the fiddle an' the bow.' An' another card said: 'Kin any good come out o' Nazareth?' meanin' East Tennessee.

"Then the mount'n in me riz big ez a mule. An' that day I made a speech. A speech fur Tennessee, with her head in the clouds an' her feet in the big Mississippi. I spoke fur the green banks uv the Wataugy an' the hills that lift ther' crested tips ter ketch alike the kiss uv sunshine an' of cloud--Fur Tennessee--the little strip God breathed upon an' Nature kissed, to set it all a-bloomin'. An' I 'lowed ez I aimed ter stan' by her, an' by her ole iron-filled hills till the breath lef' my body, spite o' coffins an' fiddles, cowbells an' tin horns. 'An' she'll stan' by me,' sez I, 'I ben't afeard ter risk ole Tennessee.' An' I give the word ez I'd never hang up the fiddle till East Tennessee ordered it, an' ole Jube Turner signed the documint. It war all in the papers nex' day an' I jest mailed 'em out ter Jube. He war mightily tickled, an' the boys all laffed some when he read it out ter they-uns.

"I made one more race, me an' the fiddle, an' hit war the stormiest race I ever set out fur. I hed a new foe ter fight this time, one ez ole Pettibrash couldn't fetch with a forty-foot pole. Hit war jist my own brother. The Republicans put him out to head me off, thinkin' ez I wuldn't make the race ag'inst my own brother. I war with Jube when the news o' the nomernation kem. An' Jube he swore an' cussed like all possessed. He give the word ez I hed to make the race fur Gov'ner o' Tennessee ef the whole fam'ly kem out ez candidates.

"I went home. I war not able ter face the ole man an' the Republican elemint i' the fam'ly; so I went out an' sot on a log under the apple tree an' watched the sun a-settin' behin' Lynn Mount'n. So, it seemed ter me, my sun war goin' down behin' the mount'n o' helplessness--my sun o' success.

"After a while my ole mother foun' me out an' kem down, an' I told her ez how I war hendered by my brother bein' a candidate. An' she heeard me out an' then--sez she-- an' her words were slow an' keerful:--

" 'Ye hev the right; Alfred knowed ez ye aimed ter mek the race, an' he hev unly done this ter hurt the Dimercrats. Ye hev the right ter go on fur yer party, the same ez Alfred hev fur his. Ye hev that right.'

"Then I riz up an' went in. An' I tuk down the old fiddle, an' teched it gentle-like, an' all the ole times kem crowdin' back. I see the Hall o' Representatives. An' I heeard the clerk's voice callin' uv the roll. An' the shouts o' the boys a-contendin'. Then it changed an' 'Hail ter the Chief,' said the fiddle in my ear, unly it war a brass band. Then the tune turned agin, an' I heeard the cowbells an' the tin horns an' the hissin' uv the people. Then it began to fade, an' then it wur a white-tail rabbit skippin' an' skeedadlin' through a turnip patch while all the world seemed ter beat time to the tune of the fiddle, singin' me to glory, an' I riz up an' shuk the fiddle in the face o' the whole house, an' sez I:--

" 'Yeas, I'll go. I will go. All hell can't hender me.'

"An' I went. Me an' the fiddle, fur it tuk tall playin' ter git above Alf, ez war up ter all my tricks.

"Nip an' tuck we run together on the first quarter, together on the second; Alf a nose behin' on the third, an' me a neck ahead on the home-stretch, me an' the fiddle. 'Fiddled himself inter the Gov'ner's cheer,' they said; an' ther' war some toler'ble tall fiddlin' done after we got ther'.

"I ain't laid her by yit, my ole pardner. Ther's a vacancy ter the United States Senate jest ahead, an'--"

There was a shout down the river: the fisherman had returned. The governor rose and shook himself.

"Ah, gentlemen," he said, "we shall have fish for our supper after all."

Richard was himself again.

AUTHOR'S NOTE.--Since this story appeared, first in the "Arena" magazine, then in a former edition of "The Heart of Old Hickory," it has called forth much pleasant speculation regarding the honorable gentleman suspected of being the hero of the sketch. The author desires to state that the story was not designed as history. Further, had she dreamed for one moment that it would have met with the generous reception that has been accorded it, she would have been careful to make this statement at the first. It is chiefly a fancy sketch with some of the characteristics of a great and good man to rest upon, as a sort of framework or foundation,--no more, nor less. W. A. D.

A WONDERFUL EXPERIENCE MEETING.

BEING Christmas time the brethren thought it not amiss that something extra, in the way of entertainment, be done at Nebo. Many and warm were the discussions before they had fairly voted down the cake-walking which the "young folks nomernated fur," the "festerble imposed " by the more worldly among the older members, and the Christmas tree espoused by those who were in the habit of carrying down presents for themselves to be "called out," while hungry-eyed little "niggers" by the score watched greedily and waited longingly, to be rewarded by a string of burnt popcorn perhaps at the last.

These being severally voted upon and put down by the more religious element, who had taken the matter in hand, an experience meeting was finally substituted in lieu of the worldly amusements, as being more in keeping with the sacred occasion. Once decided upon, all went to work alike to push it to success. Even yellow "Kelline," the belle, who always carried off the prize at the cakewalkings, rallied to the help of the " 'spe'ience meet'n' " determined to prove to the brethren that she could talk as well as walk.

It was a great meeting, a never-to-be-forgotten meeting, held Christmas morning, before sun-up; for there were the Christmas breakfasts "to be got fur de whi' folks" at the homes where many of the early worshippers were employed. They turned out in full force: Old Aunt Sally, who always nodded during the collection (wide-awake now); "Little Jinny," the fashionable member who rivalled "Kelline" in popularity; Cross-eyed Pete, the most notorious thief in the town, the most vociferous shouter in the church, and who spent at least one fourth of his time in the county jail; Old Jordan, who declared he had served his time "at bein' a nigger," and who wanted "ter git home ter

heab'n whar dey's all whi' folks dest alike;" and there was
Shaky Jake, whose idea of heaven was one of golden
streets and pearly gates, and who had never been able to
reconcile it to his conscience that so much "gold en stuff
should jes' be layin' roun' loose en doin' nuffin'." There was
"Slicky Dave" the barber, who looked upon the future bliss
as a thing of shimmer and shine and golden crowns. And
there was Uncle Mose, who had "raised the tunes " for
Nebo "sence tudder Moses lef' dar," he was wont to
declare; and who expected to be offered a seat in the choir
when he reached "de prommus lan'" and received his harp
and crown. And there was "Slow Molly," whose idea of
heaven consisted of dozing under a plum tree and waving a
palm branch. And all, from baby Jube to toothless Jake,
were to be shod in golden slippers. Heaven without those
golden slippers--oh! no; there is no such heaven possible to
the negro conception.

The morning of the big meet'n' dawned cool and crisp,
with a sprinkle of white snow, as Christmas morning
should dawn, always. "Brudder Bolles" went to work in a
manner that showed "he had Chris'mus in his bones;" brisk,
earnest, hopeful. After a short, fiery prayer he arose, and
called upon the members to speak, "to testify accord'n' ez
dey wuz moved by de Sperit ter so do."

Shaky Jake was the first to respond. "Brudder Bolles,"
said he, leaning forward, a hand thrust into each trousers
pocket, his ragged old coat a speech without words to
proclaim the fact that Christmas wasn't all warmth and
prosperity despite its cheer. But old Jake was there to
testify, not to complain. "Brudder Bolles, I hate allus
heeard say dat Chris'mus am de time fur 'spe'ience--de bes'
time ob all de times. Hit am de time when de trees bleeds,
en de cows git down on dey knees, en de sperets walks de
yearth, en de chickins en de birds don' go ter roost et all,

54

but jes' keeps watch all de night froo. So I hab heeard; en, Brudder Bolles, hit sholy am, de time. Fur las' night whilst I wuz layin' awake, thinkin' 'bout Chris'mus, en de tukkeys, en de shoat, en de poun' cake what I ud lack ter lay in fur de ole 'omen en de chillen--fur de comfut ob my fam'ly en de glory ob de Lawd-- whilst I lay dar dement'n' ob de hard times, en de col', en all, I went off into a tranch.

"En in de tranch I wuz transfloated up inter de heab'ns--jes' lack I wuz, in my ole close, hongry en po' en bent wid de mis'ry en all. En when I got dar, in my ole rags, I jes' stood et de do', 'shame' ter go in whar dey uz all dressed up in dey Sunday close en all. Look lack dey uz habbin' ob a picnic, or else dey uz all gwine on a 'scussion somewhars, dey uz all so fine, en hed so many nice fixin's. I stood afar on de outside, lookin' on. I stood, en stood swell I couldn't stan' no mo', 'count ob de col', 'ca'se hit uz Chris'mus, en winter, en all cat. I wuz jes' about ter tu'n 'way en g'long back home whar I come fum, 'ca'se I knowed I ud nuver be able ter keep up wid de style lack dey uz all containin' ob up dar, when de front do' opened en Marse Jesus Hisse'f walked out on de front peazzy. En He see me standin' afar in de col' en all, en sez He:--

" 'What's de matter, Unc' Jake? What am de incasion ob yo' bad feelin's?'

"Sez I, 'Marster, de ole nigger's mighty po' en all; en he ain't got no close fitten ter soshate wid all dem in dar!'

"He jes' step back ter de do' en retch his han' fur de bell-han'le en when de do' wuz opened, sez he ter de gyardeen ob it, sez He, 'Peter, jes' let Unc' Jake step inside dar a minit.' En I stepped in long o' Him, drappin' my ole hat on de do' step, en shadin' ob my eyes fum de glory--en a-wait'n', des' a-wait'n'.

"Well, brudderin, He jes' glanced down et dem golden streets en den up et my ole rags, en sez He, 'Unc' Jake, jes' rip up one ob de bricks out'n dat pavemint en go buy yo'se'f some close; den come up dem golden sta'rs yon'er ter de ballroom. Buy yo'se'f de wedd'n' gyarmint, fur de bridegroom sholy gwine 'specs yer ter dance et de infair ternight. En,' sez He, 'don't hab no termod'ty 'bout spendin' ob de brick, hit's yo'en, en dey's plenty mo' here, des' a-doin' nuffin'. Spen' it all; en' what's lef' go buy yo'se'f some oyschers wid hit.'

"An, den I woked up out'n de trench. En hit uz col', en de chiller uz hongry, en de breakfus' some skimp. But I'se here ter testerfy et dat ain't henderin' o' me none. Hit's warm in heab'n whar dey's all habbin' ob dey Chris'mus ter-day; Chris'mus, en oyschers, en tukkey, en all. I'll git afar bimeby, en de pavemints ull keep, 'ca'se dey's gol', en dey ain't no thief, en no mof, en no rus' fur ter cranker ob 'em. So sez I, bress de Lawd! I kin wait fur de Chris'mus ober yon'er."

Excitable "Little Jinny" sprang to her feet before old Jake had fairly taken his seat. "Brudder Bolles," she sang out in her clear, flat treble, "I rises ter gib my intestermint ter dis meet'n'. I wuz a sinner--a po', los' sinner, keerin' fur nuffin' but fine close en sech, twell I went off inter de tranch, lack de brudder what jes' spoke. En while I wuz in de tranch Marse Jesus He cum a-ridin' by in His cha'iot o' fire, wid His swode buckl't on, en His crown on His haid. En I crope out'n de paf, 'ca'se I's feard He ud jes' ride me down inter de dus', I uz sech a sinner. But He see me; He see me, en He call out ter me, 'Aw, Jinny,' sez He, 'Jinny!' En sez I, 'Yes, my Lawd.' Sez He, 'Does yer know whar yer stan's?' Sez I, 'Yes, my Lawd; I's hangin' ober hell by de ha'r ob my haid; ober de burnin' pit.' En sez He, 'Go, en sin no mo', go back ter Nebo, en tell all de brudderin I's redeemed yer.' S' I, 'Yes, my Lawd! bress de Lawd, oh my soul!' "

Yellow Kelline was not to be outdone by the startling experience of "Little Jinny."; She rose at once, a slight, nervous mulatto girl, with her handkerchief to her eyes, the graceful body in a nimble swing that kept time to the tune she unconsciously set to her words.

"Brudderin, I wuz layin' on my baid in de cool ob de mawnin', when I see Marse Jesus come ridin' by on a milk-white horse. S' e, 'How you do, Sist' Kelline?' S' I, 'I's toler'ble, thank de Lawd. How is you, Master?' S' e, 'I's toler'ble; is de folks all well?' S' I, 'Dey's toler'ble. You's all well, Marster?' S' e, 'We's toler'ble.' Den He lean down fum de saddle, en s' e:--

      " 'Whar you been, sist' Kelline,
      Dat you been gone so long?'

"S' I:--

      " 'Been a-rollin' en a prayin' et Jesus' feet,
      En my soul's gwine home ter glory.' "

"S' e:--

      " 'Keep a-rollin' en a-prayin' et Jesus' feet,
      Rollin' en prayin' et Jesus' feet,
      Rollin' en prayin' et Jesus' feet,
      My soul's gwine home ter glory. ' "

Slowly, from his seat in the Amen Corner, rose Cross-eyed Pete. The sceptic might intimate that it was the song of Kelline that suggested the thread of old Pete's experience. Be that as it may, he was none the less earnest in adding his testimony. Said he, his black face aglow:--

"Brudderin, I dreampt I wuz daid, an' et I went ter de do' o' heab'n. I went straight up ter de front do', 'ca'se de righteous am bol' ez a lion, en I wa'n't 'feard o' nuffin'. En dey ain't no sher'ff up afar ter haul a nigger off ter jail fur nuffin', neider. En when I got ter de do' I knocked; en Marse Jesus He come ter de do' His own se'f, en sez He, 'How you do, Unc' Peter?' En I tol' Him I uz des' toler'ble, en He sont me roun' ter de kitchin fur ter git wa'm. En afar wuz ole Mis' Jesus dar, 'en she gimme a cup o' wa'm coffee, en made me set down ter de side table en sot out a pone o' co'n bread, en de hock bone o' de ham what dey all hate fur de Chris'mus dinner, en de backbone o' de Chris'mus tukkey, 'stid o' sabin' ob it fur hash fur breakfus'. Den she ax me all 'bout my troubles en all, en den sez she:--

" 'Whar's you been, Unc' Peter,
Dat you been gone so long?'

"S' I:--

" 'Been a-layin' in de jail,
Wait'n' fur my bail,
En my soul's gwine home ter glory.' "

Old Jordan, fervent if rheumaticky, arose: "Brudderin en sisters! I fotches good tidin's, 'good tidin's ob gre't joy which shall be ter all people.' De book sez 'de ole men shall see vishuns.' I hab seed one. In a deep sleep, lack de same ez fell on Brudder Noey, I wuz cyar'd in a tranch up ter heab'n. When I sot my foot in de New Jerusalam my ole shoes tu'n ter gol'n slippers, en my ole close ter a white robe. My ole ha'r wuz a crown ob gol'. En de anjuls dey met me et de gate; en dey formed deyse'ves inter two lines, wid a paf down de middle fum-me ter trabul. En dey all lif' up de harps dey uz houldin' wid one hen', en de pa'm branch dey uz hould'n' wid tudder. En dey waved de pa'ms en strike de harps wid bof hen's; en dey shout, 'How you do, Brudder Jordan?' Not Unc' Jordan--naw, sah; dey ain't no Unclin' up dar. En dey say, 'Welcome home, Brudder Jordan; come en git yer harp.'

"But I sez ter de anjuls, 'Stan' out de way dar, chillun; lemme git ter de King.' En I elbowed myse'f up ter whar He uz sett'n' on de throne jest lookin' on et de glory. En He see me, en He riz up an heft out His han', en sez He, 'How you do, Brudder Jordan?' same ez de anjuls. En when He done sey dat He moved ter one side ter make room fur me, en sez He, 'Hab a seat on de throne, Brudder Jordan, en res' yose'f whil'st yo' room's afixin' fur yer.' I wuz sorter s'prised some et dat sho, en sez I, 'I's jest a nigger, sah, down yander whar I come fum.' 'Heish chile!' sez He, 'dey ain't no such word ez dat up here.' Den sez I, Marster, ef it am true lack yer sey, dat de niggers em all tu'n white up here, den what's de meanin' ob all dem colored gen'lemen stan'in' roun' here?' Sez He, 'Dey's de whi' folks what useter wuz.' Den I wuz sholy astonished, en sez I, 'Brudder, I ain't nebber heeard 'bout dat; I 'lowed we wuz all des plain white erlack.' Sez he, 'Umk-hmk! don' yer b'lieve it, honey; dey swops--dey des' swops places. See dat lean-looking nigger ober yonder by de fi'place putt'n' on a stick o' wood? Well, dat's yo ole marster what useter wuz. He's gwine put on 'is ap'n an wait on you-alls, soon's de bell rings fur dinner.' Den sez I, 'Lawd, now let dy serbent depart in peace, fur my eyes hab seen de glory.' "

Mose, the leader in song, was the next to take the witness stand. Mose made some pretensions to learning; he had a son who could read, and a grandson who was a "school-scholar" in the public schools. Mose had acquired oratory, if not English.

"Bredderin," he began, "I wuz imported, in a tranch, ter de heabenly Jerusalam. My gre't desire insistin' ob a wush ter view de glories ob de city, whenst de informalerties wuz ober I set myse'f ter de juty ob so doin'. It was suttinly a most insignifercant city ter look upon. But dat which repealed ter me de moest wuz de onpartialness ob it all. Dey wa'n't no upsta'rs en parlors fur de whi' man, wid basemints en kitchins fur de colored gent'min in dat insignificant house ob many manshens. All uz des' de same; one didn't make no mo' intentions den de tudder. De basemints uz all parlors, en de parlors uz all basemints; en afar resisted a strong fambly likeness betwixt all o' de inhabiters ob de place--a mos' strikin' insemblance.

"De wood pile hit lay et de front do', free ter der nigger en de white dest erlack. En de nigger wuz called ter de fus' table, same's as de res'. En de hin 'ouse wuz ez much for de nigger ez de white man. No mo' crop'n' roun' ter de back alley fur ter slip a chickin off'n de roos', 'ca'se de white man got too many fur his Chris'mus dinner, en de nigger got none. Umk-hmk! All dem hins, en pullets, en roosters, en fryin'-sizers. All you got ter do, jes' lif' yer hen' en yope 'em off'n de roos' same's ef yur put em dar. Umk-hmk! En de horgs en de young shoats des de same. Umk-hmk! Stan' out the way dar, chillun! Dis worl's mighty weery. But dar's Chris'mus ober yonder; chickin fixin's fur de nigger. No mo' hin roos'es all dest for the white man. Dat's all I want know 'bout heab'n'. Umk-hmk! my soul's happy, en I want to go home."

And while the Christmas bells rang out their "good tidings," who shall say that the dusky worshippers, interpreting according to their light, had not experienced a foretaste of the "great joy" promised to all men?

WHO BROKE UP DE MEET'N'?

AUNT SYLVIA told the story, as she sat on the doorstep one soft afternoon in June. She had come to return the "cup o' corn meal" she had borrowed a few days before; and while resting a moment, she related the story of the "scan'l" that had "broke up de meet'n', de big meet'n' ober at the Pisgy meet'n' house, an' tuk Brudder Simmons inter the cote, an' plumb made dey all furgit all about the feet-washin' what dey allus winds up de big meet'n' wid, ever' onct a year."

"A 'feet-washing'? What is a feet-washing, Aunt Sylvia?" I asked.

"De Lor', honey, don't you know? But den I furgit you's a Meferdis', en de feet washin's am Babtis'. De Meferdis', dey hab de fallin' fum graces instid. Well, honey, it's dis er way. De sacerment, hit's fur the cleanin' ob de soul; de feet-washin', hit's for de cleanin' ob de body."

"Ah! I see. And did the 'feet-washing' break up the meeting?" I asked, somewhat startled at this unusual interpretation of the Scriptures. She laughed; her fat, black face dropped forward, her eyes closed, her body swinging in that odd way which belongs solely to her race.

"De feet-washin' break up de meet'n'? Naw, honey, dat it didn't, dat it didn't."

"Then what did?"

"Dat's it!" she exclaimed, "dat's dest it. Dat's dest what we-all wants to know. Dat's what de cote wanted ter know; who broke up de meet'n'? Some sey hit uz Brer Ben Lytle; en some sey hit uz Brer Ike Martin; en some sey hit uz de widder Em'line Spurlock; en some sey hit uz jes' Ike's fise dorg; en den ag'in some sey hit uz de singin'; some sey de preacher hisse'f done hit; en some sey dis, en some sey dat, till dey fetches it ter de cote. En de cote figgered en figgered on it, en den it sey cord'n ter de tees' hit kin extrac' fum de eminence befo' it, wuz, dat de one ez broke up de meet'n', en oughter be persecuted en incited by de gran' jury fur de disturbmint ob de public worshup, am ole Mis' Goodpaschur's big domernicker rooster, what nobody ain't never s'picioned, case'n o' hit livin' 'way 'cross de creek, on de side todes de railroad, wid ole Mis' Goodpaschur. En de cote, hit noller prostituted de case agin de preacher, what de sisters inferred aginst him in dey charges; en dey tuk en laid hit on de domernicker instid.

"Hit uz dis erway: You see, Ike Martin, he wuz 'gaged ter chop wood fur Mis' Goodpaschur, 'count o' lett'n' uv him haul off'n her lan'. Ike, he gits a load fur ever' load he cuts. En hit 'pears in de eminence how Ike went by ter cut some wood mighty early in de mawnin', de day ob de feet-washin', 'count o' goin' ter meet'n'. En he fotched little Eli, his boy, 'long wid 'im ter pick up de chips, case'n Mis' Goodpaschur allus gibs de chile a bite o' warm bre'kfus' when he pick up de chips fur her, seein' ez Ike sent got no wife ter cook fur him. En Eli he fotched his fise dog-- thinkin' 'bout de bre'kfus', I reckin. En Mis' Goodpaschur, she axed Eli ter keep off de calf off. En while Eli, he uz wraslin' wid de calf, en nobody ain' never thought ob de domernicker up in de yeller peach tree, all 't onct afar wuz a mighty fluster up ober dey haids, en de big domernick come teetlin' en clawin' down on ter de roof ob de cow-shed wid a pow'ful healfy 'How-dy-do-oo-hoo!'

"Ole Mis' Goodpaschur, she uz dat upsot she tumbled off'n de milkin' stool, forrards agin' de cow; en de cow, she kicked little Eli in de haid, en Eli, he hollered till his daddy

63

come ter see de incasion ob de fuss. En he tell Eli ter shet up; but he say he ain' gwine shet up tell he kill dat cow; he say he 'boun' ter bus' it wide op'n.'

"En den Mis' Goodpaschur she say she sholy have him tuk up en jailed ef he tetch dat ar cow. En so Ike he tuk en tuk Eli off ter de feet-washin' fur ter keep 'im out o' mischeef.

"En de fise dog, hit went 'long too wid Eli, 'cause dat dog sho' gwine whar Eli go. En dat's jes' how it all come 'bout; ef dey all hadn't come ter meet'n', ober ter Pisgy, dey ain' been no fuss, en no scan'l, en mo talk.

"De domernick skeered ole Mis', ole Mis' skeered de cow, de cow kicked Eli, Eli hollered fur his daddy, his daddy tuk him ter de meet'n'! en dar wuz de fuss all wait'n' en raidy.

" 'Twuz de big meet'n', hit ez don't come 'cep' onct a year. Brudder Simmons wuz holdin' fo'th, en jes' a-spasticerlatin' ter de sinners en denunciat'n' ob de Scriptures. En he wuz jes' p'intedly gibbin' de gospil, bilin' hot, ter de gals en boys, de ongodly young folks ez wuz at de dancin' party down ter Owlsley's Holler de night befo'.

"Dey uz all dar, gigglin' en actin' mighty bad. En de preacher, he telled how he rid froo de Holler goin' ter Brudder Job Sawyer's house fur ter put up, en he heeard de tompin' en de singin', en he telled 'em how bad it all sound. He sey, dey uz singin' somef'n' bout "Granny, ull yo dog bite?" En he mek de p'int ter tell 'em uv dat ez'll bite more badder en any dog--it air de wraf! de wraf ter come! de fire dat'll burn, en burn, en neber stop burnin'.

"En the Chrischuns, dey wuz seyin' 'Amen!' en dest waitin' wid dey mouf wide op'n fur de trumpit ter blow fur ter start 'em all home todes de glory. En afar wuz de sinner convicted, moanin', wait'n fur de call ter resh ter de moaners' bench. En dar wuz de dancin' crown, col', col', col' ez ice, and not thinkin' ob de jedgmint day. Yes, dey wuz all dar--de worl', de flesh, en de debbul, I reckin.

"En dar wuz de moaners' bench--fur de feet-washin', hit come las'--en de moaners' bench wuz dar, stretched plumb 'crost de house, wid some clean straw throwed roun' bout'n it fur de consolerdation ob dem ez wuz come ter wras'le like Marse Jacob.

"En Ike, he uz dar, en Eli uz dar, en--de fise dog uz dar. Yes, de fise uz behavin' mighty well; a pow'ful frien'ly, onhankerous lookin' little critter, curled up on de fur eend ob de moaners' bench jes' in front ob Eli, en not seyin' a blessed word ter 'sturb nobody. En de widder Spurlock, she uz dar, in her new moanin' dress en a raid ribben in her bonnit. She done been sett'n' up ter Ike eber sence his 'oman died; en Eli, he jes' p'intedly despises de groun' she tromps on.

"Waal, den, when Brudder Simmons, he begin ter exterminate de Chrischuns ter go out inter de byways en de hedgerows, en ter furrit out de sinners en impel 'em ter come inter de gospul feast, ever'body knowed he uz talkin' 'bout de boys en gals what danced 'Granny, ull yo dog bite' all de night befo'. Ever'body knowed dat, inspectin' ob de widder Spurlock; she plumb mistuk de meanin' ob de call. Fur 'bout dat time, some ob de wraslin' ones down 't de fur eend ob de moaners' bench fum der fise, foun' grace, en begin ter claw de a'r, en ter roll in de straw like.

"De fise he looked up, much ez ter sey, 'What dat mean?'

"En den Mis' Spurlock, she jumped up, flung off her bonnit, en wen' tarin' cross de house ter whar Ike wuz sett'n' by Eli on de bench.

"Down she flopped, en flung hersef onter Ike's shoulder en begin ter holler, 'Glory! glory! Bress de Lord! I loves ever'body, ever'body, ever'--body!' en jes' poundin' Ike on de back lack same's he uz a peller, else a bolster she uz beat'n' up.

"De fise dog riz ter a sett'n' poacher, sett'n' on de hin' laigs, his tail sorter oneasy like, en his mouf workin'.

"Den I see Eli lean ober en put his mouf ter de fise's year, 'en sey, sorter easy like' sez he, 'S-i-c-k 'im!' Land o' Moses ! ef dat dog didn't fa'rly fly. He danced, en he yelped, en he barked, en he barked. He lit inter dat widder-'oman like a mad hornet. I tell yer, he made de fur fly. En den dat Eli, he jes' titled ob his haid back en laffed out loud.

"De gals fum Owlsley's Holler giggled, en de moaners peeped fum behin' dey's han'kercheefs ter see what uz de matter; en eben one ob de preachers hisse'f smiled, while Brer Ben Lytle, ez wuz kerzort'n' ob de moaners, he jes' drapped down in de straw en roared till he had ter hol' his sides, fur ter keep fum bust'n' wide op'n. Yer could a heeard him haff'n a mile, I reckin.

"Dar wuz one didn't laff; dat uz Brer Simmons. He jumped up quick ez he could, en sez he:--

" 'Sing somethin';' thinkin' ter drown out the fuss. 'Sing, bredderin! Sing dat good ole song, "Granny, will yo' dog bite." '

"En afore he could see what he had sea, dem Owlsley Holler gals set up ter singin', loud null ter raise de daid, while de boys, dey begin ter pat:--

> Chippie on de railroad,
> Chippie on de flo',
> Granny, will yo, dog bite?
> No, chile, no!

"Brudder Simmons' eyes look lack dey boun' ter pop out'n his haid; he lif' up his hen' up, so, en motion 'em ter stop. But dat only mek dey-all ter sing de more louder, en ter pat the more harder:--

> 'Possum up a 'simmon
> tree, Oh, my Joe!
> Granny, will yo, dog bite?
> No, chile, no!

"Den de Chrischuns, dey got mad. Dey 'low Brudder Simmons been et de dance his own se'f, else dat song wouldn't slip off'n his mouf so 'fly. Dey woz plumb scan'lized. Dey wuz, shore. En someun sey, out loud:-

" 'Put 'im out ! Put 'im out!' En de word uz tuk up by de whole band a' Chrischuns, exclud'n' de very moaners deyse'ves. En afore he knowed it dey jes' lit inter 'im, drug him out'n de pulpit, en pitched him out'n de meet'n house door, en shet it to, in his face, namin' ob him all de time fur a Jonah. En den dey fotched it up in de cote, persecuted ob de preacher fur disturbin' ob public worship. Dey sho' did.

"En when dey fotched it up, de preacher sey he ain' done hit. Den de cote p'intedly ax, 'Who bruk up de meet'n' ?' En some sey dis un, en some sey cat, en dey all sey dey reckin de preacher wuz de mos' ter blame--de witnesses all sey dat.

"But Brudder Simmons, he sey he didn' mean ter gib out dat song. He uz dest a-thinkin' about dat wicked dance dey-all teen habin' in de Holler, en he uz frustrated by de fise dog barkin', en when he went ter sey 'Sing dat good ole song, "Gre't God, dat awful day ob wraf,"' he forgot, en sed, "Granny, will yo' dog bite," bein' frustrated 'bout de fise en de dance.

"So den de cote axed him, 'Who bruk up de meet'n'?' En he sey ef he bleeged ter lay de blame he ud lay it ter de dog. He sey de fise dog bruk up de meet'n'. Den I gibs my intestiment, en I sey it wuzn't de dog, it uz Eli fur sickin' on de dog, 'case I heeard 'im. En Eli he sey it uz de widder Em'line Spurlock fur huggin' ob his pappy. En de widder sey it uz Ike fur fetchin' Eli ter meet'n'. En Ike sey it uz ole Mis' Goodpaschur fur tryin' ter jail Eli, else he wouldn't a-fotched de chile ter meet'n'.

"Mis' Goodpaschur sey it uz Eli, fur sayin' he 'u'd kill de cow.

"En Eli, he sey de cow uz ter blame fur kickin' uv 'im, en ole Mis' Goodpaschur fur kickin' ob de cow.

"En den ole Mis' Goodpaschur, she sey 'twuz dc domernicker crowed on de roof ez skeered her off'n de stool en made her bump ag'inst de cow.

"Now, den! de cote hit sey de eminence am all in, en it begin ter argerfy de case. En it argerfied might'ly; do de lawyers kep' a-laffin' en laffin', tell de judge shuck a stick at 'em; en he hit on de pulpit ob de cote-room wid it, en looked mighty ser'us, when his mushtash didn't shake, lack it sorter done.

"En one ob de lawyers riz up en made out de case:--

" 'De rooster crowed! ole mis' jumped ag'in' de cow; de cow kicked Eli; Eli want ter kill de cow; ole mis' want ter jail Eli; Ike fotched him ter meet'n', wid de dog; de widder hugged Ike; de dog bit de widder; de gals laffed; de preacher gin out de wrong chune; de sisters fit de preacher, en de meet'n' bruk up. En now,' sez he, ' who bruk up de meet'n'?'

"Den de judge riz up, en sez he, 'Ef de preacher hadn't gib out de wrong chune de gals wouldn't a-sung it.

" 'De preacher wouldn't done it ef de dog hadn't barked.

" 'De dog wouldn't barked ef Eli hadn't sicked 'im on.

" 'Eli wouldn't set 'im on ef de widder hadn't hugged his daddy.

" 'De widder wouldn't done dat ef he ud stayed et home wid Eli.

" 'Ef he'd stayed home wid Eli, ole Mis' Goodpaschur ud put Eli in jail.

" 'Ole Mis' Goodpaschur wouldn't do dat ef he hadn't sey he ud kill de cow.

" 'He wouldn't sey dat ef de cow hadn't kicked 'im.

" 'De cow wouldn't kicked 'im ef ole mis hadn't kicked de cow.

" 'Ole mis' wouldn't done dat ef de domernick hadn't crowed on de roof.'

"Den de judge sey, 'Wid all de eminence afore me, de exclusion reached am dat de domernicker am de culvert, en de case against de defender am noller prostituted.'

"En I sey ef de domernick am de culvert, lack he sey, den who broke up de meet'n'?"

RAGS

HIS first recollection of anything was of the Bottom, the uninclosed acres just without the city limits, the Vagabondia of the capital, and the resort of numberless stray cattle, en route to Bonedom. It was the cattle first called into active play those peculiar characteristics which marked the early career of my hero, and gave evidence of other characteristics, equally unusual, lying dormant perhaps in the young heart of him, but lacking the circumstance or surrounding of fate necessary to their awakening.

In one room of a tumble-down old row of buildings that had once gloried in the name of "Mills," our Rags was born, among the rats and spiders and vermin, to say nothing of the human vermin breeding loathsome life among its loathsome surroundings. And indeed, what else was to be expected, since life takes its color from the color that it rests upon? Just as the spring in the Bottom, where man and beast quench alike their thirst, becomes a fever-breeding pool when the accumulated filth about it gets too much for even the blessed water. It was here that Rags was born. He owed his name to his clothes, and to the kindred souls of the Bottom who had detected a fitness in the nickname, which, by the bye, soon became the only name he possessed. If he had ever had another nobody took the trouble to remember it, while as for him, he found the name good enough for all his purposes.

From the time he could use his legs well he was out among the cattle; fetching water in an old oyster cup that he had raked out from an ash heap, for such of the strays as were dying of thirst; or chasing the express trains across the Bottom, saluting with his one little rag of a petticoat the engineer on the tall trestle where the trains were constantly crossing and recrossing the Bottom; but giving his best attention always to the crippled cows and the old horses abandoned to the pitiless death of the Bottom. Any one who had chosen to study his character might have detected the humane instinct at a very early age. The instinct of justice, too, was rather strongly developed, also at an early age.

Did I say he was a negro? A mulatto with a clear olive; complexion, kinky hair, and eyes that were small and black, and showed humor and pathos and fire all in one sharp flash. He was reared in a queer school, and the lessons he learned had strange morals to them. It is no wonder they worked unusual results.

The first patient that came under Rags' ministration was an old cow which had been abandoned to the mercy of the Bottom, and which, in an attempt to return to its unworthy owner perhaps, had been caught by a passing engine and tossed from the trestle, thereby getting its back broken. Rags faithfully plied the tin cup all the afternoon, only to see at evening the poor old beast breathe its last, leaving its bones to bleach upon the common graveyard of its kind, the Bottom.

The next morning Rags' old grandmother found the boy engaged in rather a promising attempt to fire the bridge, to wreck the car, that killed the cow, that roamed the wild, that Rags ruled.

When she had pulled him away from the trestle, and had dragged him home and thrashed him soundly, what she said was, "You fool you, don't you know they'll jail you fur life if they ketch you tryin' to burn that bridge?"

If they caught him. Rags had learned shrewdness if not virtue; henceforth he resolved not to abandon rascality, but to make sure that he was not overtaken in it.

His life from the time he could remember was a series of beatings and a season of neglect. Of his mother he retained no recollection whatever; he had at a very early stage of the life-game fallen to the mercy of his grandmother and her rod. When he was not being beaten he was roaming the Bottom, along with the other stray cattle-- they of the soulless kind.

Once he remembered a party of very fine folk that had come out in carriages to look after the old horses that had been cast out by the owners they had served while service was in them. A great to-do had been made over the condition of the dumb things found there, and more than one heartless owner had been forced to carry home and care for the beast that had served him. But the little human stray that fate had abandoned to destruction--there was no humane society whose business it was to look after him. But then the cities are so full, so crowded with these little vagabond-strays; what is to be done about it?

So Rags drifted along with the fresh cattle that wandered into his domain, until one morning in January, when he awoke from sleep without being beaten and dragged from his bed for a worthless do-nothing. He sat up among the bedclothes that made his pallet and wondered what had happened. It was broad daylight; the sun streamed in at the curtainless window; while over in the city the shrill, sharp sound of whistles proclaimed the noon. In all his life he had never had such a sleep. The wonder of it quite stupefied him. He soon remembered, however, that a reckoning would be required; the wonder was that the reckoning had not already been called for. He sat up, rubbing his eyes and looking about him. Over in the corner stood his grandmother's bed; the covers were drawn up close about a figure, long, rigid, distinctly outlined under the faded covers. Sleep never yet gave a body that stiff, unreal pose--only the one sleep. The old grandmother had fallen upon that sleep.

After her death Rags found a shelter with a very old regress whom he called "Aunt Jane," a cripple, who lived over in the city, in a little den of a room off one of the chief thoroughfares, where progress was too busy to ferret out such small concerns. From the very first Rags was fond of the woman, possibly because she did not beat him.

And now it was that he began really to live. In an incredibly short time he became an expert sneak thief. The evil in him developed with indulgence. And so too--alas, the wonder of it!--did the humane. He was a strange contradiction; in color he would have been called "a rare combination." He would risk his life to rescue a child from peril, and he would risk his liberty for the penny in the child's pink fingers. He was not cruel; he had no fight against the rich. He only wanted to keep Aunt Jane and himself in food, and rags sufficient to cover their nakedness. He was not grasping; on the contrary, when he had more than was absolutely necessary for their immediate needs, he would give a bite to a less fortunate comrade of the gutters. He did not do this with any idea of show either, which cannot be said of all who give to beggars; he gave because of the humane that was a part of him; having given, he never gave the matter another thought.

He had a wonderful mind for deducing conclusions, as well as for refusing conclusions founded upon premises that were unsatisfactory to his ideas of justice.

One morning, when Rags' years had gone as far as twelve, a great circus came to the city in which fate had decreed him citizenship. Rags made one of the hundreds who followed the great procession of cages showing the painted faces of monkeys, apes, and ourang-outangs, moving majestically down the crowded street, halting now and then, as the law required, to give right of way to a passing street-car.

Following the procession, pressing close to the cages, watching the wonderful pictured monkeys, an eager, absorbed look upon his face, was a little boy. He could not have been more than six years of age, and had evidently escaped from his nurse and been crowded off the pavement into the almost equally crowded street. His rich, dainty clothing, his carefully curled, bright hair, no less than the delicate, patrician features proclaimed him a child of the upper classes. Nobody noticed him; nobody but Rags, inching along by the chimpanzees' cage. Rags' keen eye had caught the glint of silver in the little animal-lover's hand. It was the child's money to get into the circus, and which, as an inducement to manliness perhaps, he had been allowed to carry.

"Brr-rr-rr-rr!" sneered Rags. "No use o' that. Kin crope under the tent, easier'n eat'n. That's how I do." And he inched nearer, his eyes never once removed from the small, half- clinched hand holding the bit of silver. The circus was for the moment forgotten; the painted monkeys grinned on, unobserved by Rags; the lion lashed its tawny sides in malicious anticipation of a broken bar or an inadvertent lifting of the cage door; the humped-backed camels in the rear of the procession plodded along under the persuasions of the boys in orange and purple and gay scarlet mounted upon their unwilling backs. Rags was unconscious of it all--

and of the car coming down the street in a crackle and flash of electricity.

The first thing he did see clearly was a little golden head go down under the strong, lightning-fed wheels. He gave a wild, unearthly shriek and dashed to the rescue. A hundred throats took up the cry; a hundred feet hurried to help. But too late. A little motionless bundle of gay clothes and bright hair, with crimson spots upon the brightness, lay upon the track when the fiery wheels had passed. And near by lay Rags, his eyes seeing nothing, and the toes of one foot lying the other side the track.

It was months before he could hobble about again; but the very first trip he made was to limp down to the place where the accident had occurred, and, leaning against the iron fence of a yard that opened off the sidewalk, to go over the whole scene again. Had the boy escaped? he wondered; and what had become of the silver? He fancied it might be out there in the gray slush somewhere, together with his own poor toes. At the thought of them he grew faint and sick, leaning against the fence to prevent himself falling into the gutter.

While he stood thus a physician's buggy drew up to the sidewalk, and a man got out. He saw the very miserable-looking boy leaning upon a crutch and stopped.

"Are you sick?" he asked.

"No," said Rags, "I ain't sick." Then as the man was about to pass on he rallied his courage and said, "Where's the boy wuz hurt that day?"

"The boy?"

"The boy what the car runged over; where's he at?"

"Ah! The little boy that was run over the day of the circus you mean? He is dead. The car killed him. The company will have it to pay for."

Dead! The little brown face twitched nervously; the sight of it set the physician's memory twitching also.

"Now I wonder," said he, "if you are not the boy who got hurt trying to save the little fellow? That was a brave act, my boy."

There was a mist in the vagabond's eyes.

"I couldn't, though," said he. "Them wheels wuz too quick for me. They--kotched--uv--him." He drew his old sleeve across his face; he had been sick and was still weak and nervous; it was a new thing with Rags to cry.

"Never you mind," laying his hand upon the boy's head. "It was a brave, grand thing to do. It will stand for you with God some day; remember that, if you are ever in trouble. You did your best; you tried to save a fellow-being; you gave up one of your feet almost; crippled yourself for life in order to rescue another from death; and although you failed, you still did your best. That is all God cares to know; the deed stands with God for just what we mean it. He will count it for you some day, God will!"

The brown, tear-wet face looked into with a strangely puzzled expression.

"God?" said Rags, "who's God?"

"Boy, where were you brought up--not to know the good God, who watches over you, over everybody, and loves us all, and cares for us?" He paused, looked down into the knowing little old face, and wondered what manner of trick the beggar was trying to put upon him.

Suddenly the dark face lighted. Rags had turned questioner. "An' you say God sees ever'thin'? He seen the car what runged over the little kid? God wuz awatchin'? Could God 'a' stopped it?"

"Certainly."

The dark face took on the first vindictive expression it had ever worn. Rags had been asked to believe too much; the mystery of God's measures was too vast for the street child's comprehension; his conclusion was deduced only from the most humane of premises.

"Damn God," said he. "I wouldn't a let it runged over a cow, nor a dog, nor a rat; an' I ain't nothin', I ain't."

"You're a wicked sinful boy, that's what you are, and you ought to be--"

"It's a lie," said Rags stoutly. "I ain't done nothin' half as mean as God done. Psher! Damn God, I say."

"Papers? Papers? Want a paper, mister?"

The newsboy's insistent cry had to be silenced; when that was done the good man who had stopped to speak the "word in season" looked to see Rags limping down the street upon the feet maimed in humanity's cause, and quite too far away to recall. He was half tempted to get into his buggy and go after him; there was that about the boy that was strangely and strongly appealing. But he considered: "The city is full of vagabonds like him; a man cannot shoulder them all; after all nobody knows that he is really the boy he professes to be; the papers said that boy was carried off by an old negress, a cripple, nobody could tell where." Rags passed on and out of his sight forever.

The matter ended there, so far as the man knew. But Rags, hobbling down the street, gave expression to his thought with sudden vehemence.

"Somef'n's allus a-killin' o' somef'n'," said he. "Firs' it wuz a cow; then it wuz a boy; somef'n's wrong."

He had no idea wherein the wrong lay; he had never heard of Eden and the great First Cause; but he had witnessed two tragedies.

He was able to throw away his crutch after awhile, but was painfully lame, and he was never quite able to shut out the vision of a little golden head under a whirl of rushing, bfiery wheels. Another thing that he remembered was that God could have prevented the catastrophe.

With the winter Aunt Jane grew so feeble that Rags was forced to add begging to his list of accomplishments. Day in, day out, his stub toes travelled up and down the sleety pavements in search of food, and a few pennies whereby to keep a spark of fire on the hearth before which the old negress sat in her rope-bottomed chair trying to keep warmth in her pain-racked limbs.

It was Christmas day and the shops were closed; even the fruit-venders were off duty in the forenoon, so that Rags found begging a profitless employment that morning. At noon he had not tasted food since the night before, nor had old Jane. He looked in at one o'clock to rake over the ashes and hand her a cup of water. She still sat before the hearth, her feet thrust in among the warm ashes. The old face looked strangely gray and weary. Rags felt that she was starving. She looked up to say, in that half-affectionate way that had made Rags a son to her, "Neb' min', son, I ain' so hongry now; mebby someun gwine gib you a nickle dis ebenin' anyhow."

Her faith sent him out again to try for it. At three o'clock he passed a house with glass doors opening down to the street, revealing a scene which, to Rags' hungry eyes, was the most royal revelling. Some children were having a Christmas dinner-party. The table was spread with the daintiest of luxuries--oranges, grapes, and the golden bananas; cakes that were frosted like snow; candies of every kind and color. So much; so much that would never be eaten, and he asked for so little! What beggar doesn't know the feeling? Around the table a group of happy children toyed with the food for which Rags was starving; he watched them through the glass door like a hungry bear, yet not thinking of himself and his own great hunger. He was thinking how just one of those brown loaves heaped upon the side-table would put new life into the old woman at home. Had there been the slightest chance for stealing a loaf, Rags would have spent not a moment of time at the glass door more than was necessary to possess himself of the coveted feast.

He watched a white-aproned waiter carefully slice a loaf and slip a thin piece of ham between two of the narrow slices and serve to the overfed children, who nibbled a bite out of their sandwiches and threw them aside for the daintier knickknacks. The sight of the wasted food almost drove him mad. Oh, to get behind that plate glass for one moment!--for one chance at the bread which the rich man's child had thrown away! He felt as though he could have killed somebody if that would have given him the food.

Then, without warning, without any sort of volition on his part, there came to him a recollection of the man who had told him about God. Why not try if there was any truth in what the man had said? Surely God would never find a more propitious time for exercising His power. He was ignorant alike of creeds and conditions; he was simply trying God as God, and all-powerful; disrobed of all things earthy and impossible.

"God," said he, "don't you see? Don't you know they've got it all, more than they kin eat? An' don't you know Aunt Jane is starvin'? I want some of it, God! I want it fur her, fur Aunt Jane. Give it to me. He said you kin give it to me, God. God! God! God! I say, give it to me, fur Aunt Jane."

As the crude petition ended the aproned waiter stepped to the side-door with a plate of scraps in his hand and whistled softly to a little terrier dog that came frisking up to get them. The man had no sooner disappeared within the door than Rags seized upon the cast-out bits. The dog resented the intrusion upon his rights in a low growl that brought the waiter to the door again. Rags made one dash for the precious heap before he disappeared around the corner. Safe out of sight he took an inventory of his possessions; half a slice of bread, a filbert, a lemon-rind, a banana with a spoiled spot on one end, and a half-eaten pickle. A pitiful mixture for which to risk his liberty, but his heart beat with jubilance that found expression in words as he hurried off home with his treasures:

"I got it, anyhow," he was mumbling. "You wouldn't git it fur a pore ole nigger as wuz starvin', but I got it, Mr. God; I stole it fum the dogs."

The maimed foot came down upon a bit of ice that must have brought him to the ground with a smart thump but for a hand that was put out to stay him--a strong, safe, woman's hand; the hand of a lady; white, soft, bejewelled. It rested for a moment upon Rags' tattered old sleeve; the velvet of her wrap brushed his cheek. In all his hard little life he had never felt anything like it. There was about her that presence of cleanliness which attaches to some women like a perfume.

"Are you hurt, little boy?" she asked.

At the voice's sweetness the dark eyes lifted to hers suddenly filled with tears. Like a far-off gleam of light it came to him that, after all, there might be a side of humanity with which he had never come in contact; a something responding to something within himself, deep down, unknown, unnamed, like the glorious possibilities slumbering unchallenged within his own benighted little soul.

The owner of the voice stood looking down a moment at the queer, silent little figure, the rags, with the tawny-brown skin showing through, the maimed foot, and the tears which the little beggar staunchly refused to let fall. She was young and beautiful; she belonged to God's great army of good women whom the less philanthropic are pleased to denominate "cranks."

"What is your name, boy? " she asked, releasing the tattered sleeve.

"Rags."

The pathos of the reply, and the name's great fitness, appealed to her more than any beggar's plea he could have framed.

She thrust her hand into the pocket of her velvet wrap and took from it her purse.

"You are to buy yourself something to eat, and then you are to come to me--there. Anybody can show you the place."

She placed a half-dollar and a white visiting card in his hand, and passed on before Rags could fashion a reply; even had there been anything for him to say. His usually nimble tongue had no words for the great event that had come into his life, but the quick brain had opened to receive a thought--a thought which, like fire, carried all his fierce doubts before it.

"He heard me! He heard me!--God did."

It had come direct, swift, certain. And the knowledge of prayer answered thrilled him with a strange, sweet awe that was almost fearful in its intensity. The man had spoken truly; there was a God; He had given him food and help for Aunt Jane. Ah! He was a good God, though He let the little boy be killed; perhaps he should know why some day, when he came to know Him better. He would have many things to ask Him, many things to tell Him--this good God that kept them from starving. He had not thought to throw away the scraps he had taken from the dog nor stopped to buy the dinner of which he stood in such sore need. The knowledge of food possible had served to blunt the edge of hunger. He only wanted to get home with his wonderful news, to get a bite for Aunt Jane; and then by and by, when she could spare him, he would find the lady.

He pushed open the door and entered, calling the good news as he went. The old negress was sitting just as he had left her in the big chair before the fireless hearth. She neither moved nor spoke, but sat with her head leaned back against the chair, mouth open, and the sightless eyes staring, unseeing, away into that mystery where none might follow. Instantly he recognized that she was dead. He stood looking at her in awe, stricken, silenced, frightened; not at death but at life, which he began to understand was something too deep and vast and terrible for him. It was the second time that death had met him thus, the third time they two had faced each other without warning or preparation. The persistency with which it seemed to trail and pursue him sent a kind of superstitious thrill through him. What a tragedy in a nutshell his life had been!

He glanced from the changed, dead face to his full, clinched hands, and slowly his fingers opened. The silver rang upon the hearth bricks and disappeared quickly in the fireless white ashes, as though fleeing from the new presence in the room. The broken bits of food lay upon the floor at the dead woman's feet, and the lady's white visiting card fell, face up, forgotten, as with a wild cry Rags turned and fled--away from death, away into the ice-crusted, frozen street; away from life and its too mysterious meaning.

A wagon was coming down the street as he tried to cross, and in his haste he tripped and fell. He heard the driver's startled shout to the horses, but he did not know when the wagon passed over him. The crowd that gathered was not altogether drawn by curiosity to see the little maimed body of a child among the slush and ice of the street. A lady in velvet was picking her way through the frozen mud, giving directions to the driver of the team.

"Carry him in there," she commanded, pointing to the door Rags had left wide open. "I saw him run out of there; I was following him. Then do some of you men run for the hospital wagon, quick--don't stand there staring, you may need it yourselves some day. Be easy with him, my man, there is life there yet."

Within the room to which they bore him, an old woman's dead face, lifted to the sooted ceiling with a kind of defiant triumph, met them; half hidden by the white ash upon the hearth a piece of coldish gray silver seemed to be spying upon their movements; and at the feet of the dead a bit of white cardboard, bearing the marks of a child's soiled fingers, lay turned up to catch the winter sun streaming through the uncurtained window; the black letters seemed to catch a radiance of their own:

Isabel Gray.
The Woman's Relief Society. 72 N.
Summer.

When Rags opened his eyes in the hospital they rested upon a lady, richly dressed, standing at his bedside. She saw the recognition in the wide, wondering eyes, and stooping, spoke his name:

"Rags?"

"Yessum," said Rags, "yessum, I hears yer, Miss Lady."

"Boy," she began, startled, and afraid that the struggling life might slip before she could deliver her message to the wanderer--"boy, do you know who sent me to you?"

Under its cuts and bruises the dark face glowed.

"Yessum," said Rags, "hit wuz God. Dat ar white man say God ud count it up fur me, an' I reckin He done it."

She hadn't the least idea what he was talking about, but she understood that someone had dropped a seed. Slowly the beautiful head drooped forward, the lips moved softly, but with no sound that could reach beyond the ear of God:--

"Lord, if I might rescue one, but one, of Thy poor wandering race!"

OLE LOGAN'S COURTSHIP.

OLE Loge he's been a-courtin'.

Naw!

Is, now. He tol' big Si, his uncle, an' big Si he tol' little John, his nevvy, an' little John he tol' me. Little John woz comin' down the road f'm his place, j'inin' mine on yon side, an' I met him--jest like I met you bit ago, comin' up I'm your, j'inin' mine on t' other side--an' him an' me we sot ourse'ves on the rail fence here jest like me an' you're doin' of now; an' little John he wuz pow'ful tickled about somethin'. I didn't know at first that thar loose-j'inted, hide-bound, bean-pole figger of Loge Beaseley wuz passin' down t' the crossroads yander. Little John he begin to whittle a cedar splinter, like I'm a-doin', an' whilst he wuz whittlin' uv the cedar he tol' me about ole Loge's gain' a-courtin'.

An' little John he said the firs' thing Loge had to git his own consent to wuz the makin' of his mind up. When that wuz done the worst wuz over--so Logan allowed. But shucks! it wuz no more en half, if Logan hadn' been sech a blamed fool not to know it. But you see, bein' ez it had took Loge nigh about forty year to make up his mind to go court'n' it seemed sort o' big when he got it made up, naturly.

An' his ma, ez thinks to this good minute Loge's wearin' knee pants an' caliker jackets --when he tol' his ma 'bout his aimin' to git married, the ole lady jest bust out a-cryin' and said she wuz afeard he wuz too young to know how to choose, an' hadn't he better put it off a spell till she could look about fur him?

But Loge allowed he had about made up his mind it wuz to be one o' the Sid Fletcher gals, though he ain't no ways made up his mind as to which un. Then little John said as how his ma took on mightily, and said the Sid Fletcher gals wouldn't do no ways in the worl' 'count o' their pa bein' an unbeliever. She wuz afeard it might be in the blood.

But Loge he helt out fur the Sid Fletcher gals, so little John say, and went upstairs to black his boots. They wuz his Sunday boots, an' they ain't been wore much since ole Miss Hooper died, in the Cripple Creek neighborhood, two years back. An' his ma, sett'n' downstairs an' hearin' the blackin' box whackin' back into its place on the floor ever' time Loge took the bresh out'n it, she smiled like an' begin to wonder ef 't be Miss Mary, though she 'lowed it might be Mandy; it couldn't in reason be that thar frisky little Jinnie.

Then she hoped to goodness Loge's wife ud be a knitter. Loge ud need some un to knit his socks when she wuz gone; an' some un to darn 'em, too, for she say there wa'n't another man in middle Tennessee as hard on his socks, solittle John said Loge's ma said, as Loge Beaseley. An' as fur clean socks, Mis' Beaseley allowed there hadn' been a Sunday mornin' since Loge took to sleepin' upstairs, stid o' in the trundle bed in her room, that she ain't been obleeged to fetch his socks up to his door and wait there to git his s'iled ones; Loge bein' that furgitful he ud put on one clean un an' one s'iled un, or one white an' one red, maybe, or else jest put on both the same ole s'iled uns ag'in an' sen' the clean uns back to the wash-tub.

Loge's bashful, you know, mighty skeery o' women. Ain't never looked at a gal on Cripple Creek, barrin' the Sid Fletcher gals. He had opened uv the big gate onc't fur Mandy when she rid a buckin' horse to meet'n, an' the blamed critter jest wouldn't side up to the gate so's she c'u'd reach the latch.

An' onc't when there wuz a camp-meet'n' over in the Fox Camp neighborhood, what they useter have ever' onc't a year, Loge he wuz there. An' he passed a hymn book to that pretty little Jinnie o' the Sid Fletcher gang. The pars'n he axed Loge to pass the books roun', and Loge done it. Little John say he handed her in an' about sevin books, bein' that flustrated he didn't know there's anybody else at the meet'n', after Jinnie smiled, an' said, "Thank you, sir, I've got a book," ever' time Loge offered her another.

All the folks wuz smilin' too, but he didn't know it; he didn't know he had set his big foot down on Jinnie's new cloth gaiter, or that he had clear furgot to turn back the hem o' his pantaloons that he had turned up in crossin' the creek on the rocks, havin' walked over to camp 'count o' his ma havin' rid the sorrel mare over on Sadday, her havin' to fetch a lot o' victuals an' sech fur Sunday. An' he didn't know ez he'd wore one red sock an' one white un; his ma not bein' there to see ez he got fellows. An' little John say there wuz the fool a-poppin' up an' a-dodgin' up an' down the meet'n' house with three inches o' red a-shinin' up on un leg, betwixt shoe an' pantaloons, an' three inches o' white on t'other--just like a jockey at a race track or a fool clown in a circus fur all the worl'.

An' little John say to cap it all, an' clap the climax, there wuz a long white string adodgin' Loge's lef' heel all roun' the meet'n' house, makin' ole Loge look like one o' these here wooden limber jack fellers that run up a stick an' double theirse'ves inter a knot ef you pull a string. That's what little John say. An' ever'body wuz a-laffin', an' Jinnie she wuz snickerin' behin' her hymn-book, fur ever' time she smiled Loge he'd come ajouncin' back to poke another book at her.

But lor, ole Loge allowed all them smiles wuz jest 'count o' him; an' little John say that's how come he first got that fool notion about goin' a-courtin.' Little John say ole bach'lors are sech blamed fools, an' so stuck on theirse'ves, they thinks if a woman looks at 'em they're breakin' their necks to marry of 'em.

So ole Loge he got it into his head to git married. Though he wa'n't settled in his min' as to which o' the gals he'd take. He wuz kind o' stuck on the whole gang, little John say. An' Loge say he owed it ter all o' 'em to marry 'em, he wuz 'feard. Now, there wuz Miss Mary, the oldest one; little John say Loge foun' a guinea nes' onc't in the corner o' the fur eend fence what divides their two plantations. 'Twuz some time in May; there wuz twenty odd eggs in the nes' when Loge found it. Little John say Loge knowed it wuz a guinea nes' 'count o' the old guinea hen bein' a-sett'n' on it whenst he foun' it. An' the fool skeered her off; she didn't want to git off much, but Loge made her. He punched her with a fence rail till he broke three eggs; but he got her druv off at last.

An' then he picked up the eggs in his hat an' fetched 'em up to the house, allowin' they must be Miss Mary's, bein' es they wuz on her side the fence; and bein', too' as Miss Mary wuz the housekeeper an' 'tended to the chickens an' things, her ma bein' knocked up with rheumatism fur the last endurin' five years. So Loge he fetched the eggs up in his hat, mighty keerful not to break a single one. He tromped across the clover bottom, two corn fiel's, a cotton-patch, an' a strip o' woods lot, barcheaded, in the blazin' sun; little John say his bald head look like a b'iled beet with the skin took off when he got to the kitchen door an' give the eggs to ole Aunt Cindy, the cook, askin' her to give 'em to Miss Mary fur him.

Ole Aunt Cindy she looked sorter skeered like, a minute, an' then she gin a grunt, but she ain't sayin' nothin' till Loge uz gone home. Then she walked out the back door an' flung them guinea eggs over in the hog lot. Then she went in the house an' tol' Miss Mary ole Logan Beaseley done broke up the guinea nest they wuz lookin' fur to hatch out nex' day. She say there wuz twenty-one little dead guineas layin' over in the hog lot, all just ready to hop out o' their shells.

Miss Mary didn't say much--she's allus mighty quiet an' sober an' dignified; but Mandy, the second gal, she flared up an' allowed a fool-killer would be a mighty welcome vis'tor to that neighborhood, that he would. An' Jinnie, the young, pretty one, she jest laffed out, fit to kill, an' asked Aunt Cindy if she couldn't have scrambled guineas fur breakfast.

Ole Logan wuz bewitched, I reckin. Little John says he wuz conjured. He didn't know which o' the gals he ud take, but he tol' his ma he felt obligated to marry one o the Sid's 'count o' havin' paid 'em consider'ble notice--meanin' the big gate, the hymn-book, an' the guinea eggs--an' folks ad be ap' to talk if he didn't. Besides, the gals would expect it, an' feel sorter slighted if he didn't marry into the fam'ly.

Him an' Sid wuz good frien's. He had borrowed Sid's chilled plow onc't when his own wuz at the blacksmith's an' the river riz so's he couldn't go fur it. An' Sid had borrowed Loge's steelyards onc't to weigh some cotton, before sendin' of it off to the gin. He didn't visit anywheres else much, outside o' funer'ls an' meet'n's at the church.

91

So he set off on the sorrel; that little runt of a mare with the sway back, an' a tail that the calf chawed off one night when Loge put the calf up in the stable along o' the mare, so's to keep it from chawin' up the saddle blanket hangin' in the back po'ch. Little John say his uncle met Loge comin' up the lane on the sorrel. He say he knows ole Noah took that little swayback in the ark with him, 'count o' it bein' little like, an' its back makin' a good seat fur his grandchillen to ride on.

An' he say that Cripple Creek wuz right smart up, an' ole Loge had to hol' up his long legs to keep 'em out the water, 'count o' havin' on his best Sunday pantaloons; spankin' new ones to go courtin' in. So Loge he hitched his feet up behin' him, g'inst the swayback's flanks, an' plumb forgot to take 'em down any more, but rid right up to the gate with his legs hunked behin' him, like a grasshopper ready fur to jump.

He seen the gals at the winder, all smilin' a welcome, as Loge thought, an' again he begin to wonder, which one he orter take. He tied the sorrel to a hick'ry limb an' went on up todes the house.

The house has got a new wing made o' log; it ain't quite finished yit, an' there's two front doors. Loge couldn't fur the life uv him tell which door he orter take, an' he begin to git orful skeered that minute. He went on, though, bekase he see he couldn't make it back to the sorrel without passin' the winder again; an' he allowed to his uncle, big Si, as how he'd a ruther died as to a parsed that there winder again. So he plunged right on, inter the wrong door, an' run into the gals' room where Miss Mary wuz sort'n' out clean clothes, 'count o' it bein' Sadday evenin'.

When she looked up from the pile o' petticoats she woz count'n' an' see that figger o' Loge's in the door, she jest riz right up, an' says she, kind o' fierce like, "Father's down in the cornfiel'; you can go down there, or I'll ring the bell fur him."

Loge he begin to twist his coat-tails; they wuz already half way up to his armpits, so little John say, an' little John say he reckin he clear furgot about havin' come a-court'n', fur says he, "No'm; no, Miss Mary, you needn't ring the ole man up--I jest called by over here to--to--er"--he saw a cedar pail on the shelf in the open passage-way betwixt the back end part o' the house, the dinin' room an' kitchen, an' the front part where the fam'ly lives, an' that cedar pail wuz the savin' uv him--"I jest come over here," says he, " to git a goad o' water."

An' Miss Mary she stepped to the passage with him, an' p'inted first to the pail on the shelf an' then to the wellsweep down in the yard, an' says she, "There's the pail; it's full an' fresh, but if it ain't enough to satisfy your thirst, yonder's the well."

Loge allowed to his uncle as he decided right there he wouldn't choose Miss Mary he begin to see she didn't suit him. He say he wuz afeard she couldn't darn socks.

It was jest when Loge lifted the goad to his mouth that Jinnie she called out to Miss Mary from her ma's room, an' sez she:--

"Sister Mary, ma says you're to fetch Mr. Beaseley right in here to the fire "--the ole 'omen keeps a fire goin' winter an' summer, 'count o' the rheumatiz--"she says she knows he's mortal tired after his thirsty ride."

Rid four miles fur a goad o' water; cross Cripple Creek three times, an' Pant'er twicet, to say nothin' o' Forkid Branch that winds in an' out an' up an' across them too plantations like a moonstruck chicken snake tryin' to foller out the corporation line o' them Tennessee towns what hev been down with the boom fever, an' ain't made out to set itself straight yit! That sharp little Jinnie seen through that; excuse in half a minute an' that's why she called out to Loge to come in.

But little John say the fool ain't no more'n heard her voice than the goad went whack to the floor like a sky rocket on the home run.

"You're to come right in, Mr. Beaseley," says Jinnie, "an' you're to put your horse in the barn first, if you please, because pa's got a new heifer cow that's had to be turned in the yard to keep her out o' the cornfiel'. An' she's that give to chewin' things Aunt Cindy has to dry the clean clothes in the kitchen to keep her from eat'n' us all clean out of a change. She's e't up two tablecloths an' a sheet, three petticoats an' a brand new pair o' my sister Mary's stockin's. She'll eat your saddle flaps teetotally off if you leave your mare out there."

Ole Loge he looked foolish; the yearlin' at home had gnawed them saddle skirts into sassage meat long ago. He put his horse up, though, in the barn--the big barn what opens on to the lane. An' little John say the blamed fool forgot ter shut the barn door, an' the mare walked out same time Loge did, an' walked right on back home.

Well, little John say it begin to rain todes dark, an' the ole man he tol' Loge he mus' stay all night; an' Loge he done it. You see, they built up a right peart fire, 'count o' rheumatic an' rain, an' they give Loge a seat in the cornder.

94

An' when black-eyed Mandy axed him if he didn't think a sprinklin' now'n' then wuz healthy, he bein' Methodist, ole Loge got that skeered he made a lunge at the big iron shovil an' begin to twist it roun' an' roun', an' to say he didn't know but what 'twas! Then he begin to jab his fingers through the iron ring at the end o' the shovil handle; an' he kep' that up till he got to his thumb; an' hit went through all right, but it stuck. Loge he got plumb skeered then; twis' an' screw as he would, the darn thing wouldn't budge. So when ole man Sid axed him to stay all night he said he would, bekase you see he couldn't go home nohow if he'd a mind to 'less he carried the shovil, too.

An' then the supper bell rung, an' the ole man' bid 'em all out to supper; but Loge he said he wouldn't choose any-- he wuzn't a mighty hearty feeder at night, count o' dreams. An' little John say the folks went out an' left him, an' bein' left to hisse'f he set about gittin' loose. He tried an' he tried; an' at last he made up his min' to sneak out the front door and cut out fur home, shovil an' all. Then he remembered he'd orter licked his thumb, an' he tried that, but it wouldn't go. Just as he got up to tiptoe out, the shovil hangin' on like a partner at a picnic, an' 'bout the time he'd walked half across the room, the blamed thing slipped off'n that licked thumb o' Loge's, an' struck the hard floor like a clap o' young thunder.

Loge he jumped like a trounced frog, an' give one skeered little beller, like a Durham bull with the hiccups.

Before the family went in to supper Loge he'd made up his mind, in an' about, as it mus' be Mandy. It appeared 's if that 'ud be more gratifyin' to his ma, as Mandy seemed turned religious, talkin' o' Methodists an' sech. But when that shovil drapped an' Loge bellered out like he done, an' he heard Miss Mandy come out into the passage an' call out to Jube, the hired man, that big Buck, ole Sid's yeller steer, wuz in her ma's room breakin' up things, Loge say he set it right down to hisse'f as she wouldn't do fur a farmer's wife- -not knowin', like she done, that steers wouldn't come up into a house an' desturb things, not fur nothin'. He say farmers' wives mus' learn better'n that.

So little John say that Loge made choice o' Jinnie. An' Jinnie she seemed mighty willin', bein' young an' gayly. An' she set her cheer up close to Loge's an' talked mighty polite to him after supper. She tol' him he ought to git married, an' have a wife to look after his socks an' things. An' she axed mighty kind about his ma, an' got it all out o' Loge 'bout his ma want'n' him to wait till he wuz older, an' all that.

An' them two talked on till Miss Mary got up an' went off to bed; an' Mandy went out in the kitchen an' set with ole Aunt Cindy; an' ole Sid an' his wife went sound asleep in the chimbly cornders, an' didn't wake up till the clock wuz strikin' twelve. Then the ole man lit a light an' showed Loge off into the new room, hit being the only spare room in the house, an' hit not finished. As I wuz sayin' the daubing wuzn't all in, nor all the chinkin'; but bein May, an' Loge healthy, the ole man ruminated as that didn't matter much.

But he tol' Loge as he'd better blow out his candle before he undressed if he wuz afeard o' bein' seen through the cracks. An' Loge done it, an' when he had done it he couldn't find a cheer to hang his Sunday pantaloons on. He felt all over the room, mighty keerful, but he couldn't find no cheer. He wa'n't gain' to hang them new breeches on the bare floor, that was mighty certain. An' he wuz afeard to hang 'em on the foot o' the bed, count o' it bein' low, an' they wuz likely to be rumpled, too, Loge bein' considerable of a kicker. So he jest smoothed the pantaloons out keerful an' laid 'em, longways, between two o' the logs o' the house, where the chinkin' ort to 'a' been. Little John say Loge tol' big Si he felt like it wuz a young baby he wuz layin' by to sleep, he wuz that partic'lar not to wrinkle up his breeches. An' ten minutes after he put 'em there he wuz sound asleep betwixt two o' Miss Mary's best sheets.

It wuz sun-up when old Loge woke up' an' the ole man wuz callin' him to breakfast. Loge called back he'd be there in a minute, an' he begin to hustle about to dress hisse'f. He reached fur his pantaloons--then he stopped still, like the blame blockhead that he is. They wuz gone! clean gone! He searched on the floor, an' he flung off the bed clothes to look there; he got down on his hands an' knees to look under the bed. He even tore open Miss Mary's bureau drawer to see if he didn't git up in his sleep an' cram 'em in there. Then he felt down his long legs to see if he mightn't forgot an' kep' 'em on. Naw, sir; nothin' there but skin an' bone-bare carcass. He scratched his head an' tried to think; they wuz sho'ly round somewheres; he had jist forgot, in one o' his absent-minded fits, an' laid 'em somewheres. He looked behin' the door, an' on top the wardrobe, an' under the bed again; he pulled all the gal's things out o' the bureau drawers an' shook 'em up piece by piece; he looked in the slop bucket, an' behin' the washstan'; he raked out the cedar bresh the gals had decorated the fireplace with an' looked there; he stuck his head up the chimbly an' looked there; then he tuk it out again, kivered with soot an' ashes, an' went back to bed, an' give out that he wuz mighty sick, an' would some un please go fur his ma.

An' little John say his ma come over terrectly, but she went home again in a minute; jouncin' up an' down on the swayback sorrel like a house afire. An' little while later she rid over agin with a bundle tied to the side-saddle; an' after while ole Loge he watched fur a chance when there wa'n't nobody lookin' to sneak off through the woods an' go home.

He'd made up his mind not to marry yit; Jinnie she wuz young, an' could wait a bit.

An' little John say, that later in the day Jinnie she was nosin' about in the yard to see if her rose-bushes wuz putt'n' out proper' an' she see the new heifer cow a munchin' mighty contented like, on a little pile o' truck that looked like carpet rags. An' she got a fishin' pole an' fished it up, an' looked at it, laffin' fit to kill all the time. Then she called to the gals to come there quick; an' when they come says she,--

"Here's what ailed him-here's why he didn't want no breakfast, an' here's why his ma made them two trips this mornin'."

Then Miss Mandy she say she'd like to know what that roll o' strings got to do with the clothes bein' all flung out o' the drawer. An' little Jinnie say she reckin ole Loge wuz lookin' to see if he could find anything 'mongst Miss Mary's clothes as would fit him, so's he could come to breakfast.

"Bekase," says she, "these are bound to be his breeches. I know it's breeches, by the buckles; the cow ain't chawed them past identifyin'."

Then little Jinnie she laffed mightily, an' tol' the others she'd a good min' to send the things home with her compliments.

An' the next week I got a bid to the weddin' of Jinnie an' little John.

Yes, sir, ole Loge he went a-courtin'; he tol' big Si, his uncle, an' big Si he tol' little John, his nevvy, an' little John he tol' me.

And the man on the rail fence chuckled, and went on carefully whittling the last of his cedar splinter.

THE HEART OF THE WOODS.

TWILIGHT fell softly over Beersheba' beautiful Beersheba. It is going into history now with its sad old fancies and its quaint old legends, its record of happiness and of heartbreak,--those two opposing, yet closely interwoven, inevitables which always belong to a summer resort.

But Beersheba is different from the rest, in that the railroads have never found it; and it goes into history a monument to the old days when the wealthy among the southern folk flocked to the mountains, and to Beersheba-- queen of the hill country of Tennessee.

The western sky, where it seems to slope down toward Dan, had turned to gaudy orange; the east was hazy and dimly purple, streaked with long lines of shadow, resembling, in truth, some lives we remember to have noticed, lives that for all their royal purple were still blotched with the heavier shadows of pain that is never spoken.

It was inexpressibly lonely; a cowbell tinkled in the distance, and now and then a fox barked in a covert of Dark Hollow, that almost impenetrable jungle that lies along the "Back Bone," a narrow zigzag ridge stretching from Dan to Beersheba.

Dan, modest little Dan, seven furlongs distant from queenly Beersheba, with its one artistic little house, refusing in spite of time and weather, and that more deadly foe, renters, to be other than pretty and picturesque, as it nestles like a little gray dove in its nest of cedar and wild pine. A very dreamful place is Dan, dreamful and safe.

Safe; so thought the man leaning upon the low fence that inclosed the old ante-bellum graveyard that was a part of Beersheba also. For in the olden days people came by families and family connections, bringing their servants and carriages. And those who died at Beersheba were left sleeping in the little graveyard--a quiet spot, shut in by old cedars and rustling laurel. A very solemn little resting-place, with the cedars moaning, and the winds soughing, as if in continual lament for the dead left to their care. Among the quiet sleepers was one concerning whom the man leaning upon the fence never tired of thinking, while he made, by instinct, it seemed to him, a daily pilgrimage to her grave. It was marked by a long, narrow shaft, exceedingly small at the top. Midway the shaft a heart, chased out of the yellow, moss-stained marble, a heart pierced by a bullet. He had brushed the moss aside long ago to read the quaint yet fascinating inscription:--

"Millicent--April, 1862.

'Oh, Shiloh! Shiloh!' "

He had heard the story of the sleeper underneath often, often. It is one of the legends, now, of Beersheba. Yet he thought of it with peculiar interest, that twilight time, as he stood leaning upon the low fence while the sun set over Dan. His face, with the afterglow of sunset full upon it, was not a face in keeping with the quiet scene about him. It was not a youthful face, although handsome. Yet the lines upon it were not the lines made by time: a stronger enemy than time had left his mark there. Dissipation was written in the ruddy complexion, the bloated flesh, and the bloodshot eye. The continual movement of the hand feeling along the whitewashed plank, or fingering, unconsciously, the trigger of the loaded rifle, testified, in a dumb way, to the derangement of the nervous system which had been surrendered to that most debasing of all passions, drink. He had sought the invigorating mountains, the safety of isolation, to do for him that which an abused and deadened will refused to do. It is a terrible thing to stand alone with the wreck of one's self. It is worse to set the Might-Have-Been side by side with the Is, and know that it is everlastingly too late to alter the colorings of either picture.

His was an hereditary passion, an iniquity of the father visited upon the son. Against such there is no law, and for such no remedy.

He thought bitterly of these things as he stood leaning upon the graveyard fence. His life was a graveyard, a tangle of weeds, a plat of purposes overgrown with rank despair. He had struggled since he could remember. All his life had been one terrible struggle. And now, he knew that it was useless, he understood that the evil was hereditary, and to conquer it, or rather to free himself from it, there was but one alternative. He glanced down at the rifle resting against his knee. He did not intend to endure the torture any very great while longer. He possessed the instincts of a gentleman,-- the cravings of a beast. The former had won him something of friends and sympathy, --and love. The latter had cost him all the other had won. For coming across the little graveyard in a straight line with the shadows of the old cedars, her arms full of the greens and tender wild blossoms of the mountain, was the one woman he had loved. She had done her best to "reform" him. The world called it a "reform." If reform meant a new birth, that was the proper name for it, he thought, as he watched her coming down the shadow-line, and tried to think of her as another man's wife; this woman he loved, and who had loved him.

He saw her stop beside a little mound, kneel down, and, carefully dividing her flowers, place the half of them upon a child's grave. Her face was wet with tears when she arose, and crossing over to the tall, yellow shaft, placed the remainder of the offering at its base. She stood a moment, as if studying the odd inscription. And when she turned away he saw that the tears were gone, and a hopeless patience gave the sweet face a tender beauty.

" 'Oh, Shiloh! Shiloh!' "

He heard her repeat the melancholy words as she moved away from the old shaft, and opening the gate he waited until she should pass out.

"Donald!"

"I couldn't help it, Alice. You are going away to-morrow; it is the last offence. You will forgive it because it is the last."

"You ought not to follow me in this way it isn't honorable. See! I have been to put some flowers on my little baby's grave." She glanced back, as she stood, her hand upon the gate, at the little flower-bedecked grave, where, two months before, she had buried her only child.

"You shared your treasures with the other," he said, indicating the tall shaft.

"I always do," said she. "There is something about that grave that touches me with singular pity. I feel as if it were myself who is buried there. I think the girl must have died of a broken heart."

"Have you never heard the story?" said Donald. "I suppose it might be called a broken heart, although the doctors gave it the more agreeable title of 'heart disease.' It is very well for the world that doctors do not call things by their right name always. Now, if I should be found dead to-morrow morning in my little room at Dan, the doctors would pronounce me a victim of 'apoplexy,' or 'heart failure.' That would be very generous of the doctors so far as I am concerned But would it not be more generous to struggling humanity to say the truth? 'This man died of delirium tremens,-- killed himself with whiskey. Now you other sots take warning.' "

"Donald Rives!" the sad eyes, full of unspoken pity, not unmixed with regret, sought his.

"Truth," said Donald. "And truth, Alice, is always best. The world, the sick moral world, cannot be healed with falsehood. But the woman sleeping there--she has a pretty story. Will you wait while I tell it--you are going away to-morrow."

She glanced down the road, dim with the twilight.

"The others are gone on to Dan, to see the moon rise," she said hesitatingly.

"We will follow them there in a moment," said Donald. "I have a fancy for telling you that story."

He laughed, a nervous, mirthless kind of laugh, and slipped his rifle to his other hand.

"She had a lover in the army, you understand. She was waiting here with hundreds of others until 'the cruel war should cease.' One day when there had been a great battle, a

104

messenger came to Beersheba, bringing news for her. He brought a letter, and she came across the little court there at Beersheba, and received it from the messenger's own hand. She tore it open and read the one line written there. Then the white page fluttered to the ground. She placed her hands upon her heart as if the bullet had pierced her. 'Oh, Shiloh! Shiloh!' That was all she said or did. The ball from old Shiloh did its work. The next day they buried her up there under the cedars. The letter had but one line: 'Shot at Shiloh, fatally;' and signed by the captain of the company who had promised to send news of the battle. Just a line; but enough to break a heart. Hearts break easily, sweetheart."

She looked at him with her earnest eyes full of tears.

"Do you think hers broke?" she asked. "I do not. She merely went to him."

"As I should go to you if you were to die, because I cannot live without you."

"Hush! I am nothing to you now. Only a friend who loves you, and would help you if she could, but she is powerless."

"O Alice, do not say that. Do not give me over in that hopeless way to ruin. Do not abandon me now."

"Donald," the voice was very low, and sweet, and--strong. "There was a time I thought to help you. I did my best and--failed. It is too late now. I am married. You, who could not put aside your passion for the girl whose heart was yours, and whom you loved sincerely, could not, assuredly, put it by for the woman whose love, and life, and duty are pledged to another. Yet, you know I feel for you.

You know what it is to be tempted, so, alas! do I. Wait! stand back. There is this difference. You know what it is to yield; but I have that little mound back there"--she nodded toward the little flower-decked grave--"the dead help me, the sleeper underneath is my strength. If I were dead now, I would come to you, and help you. Do that which, living, I failed in doing. Come, now; let us go on and see the moon rise over Dan. The others have gone long ago."

They passed out, and the little gate swung to its place. The dead at Beersheba were left alone again. Left to their tranquil slumbers. Tranquil? Aye, it is only the living who are eager and unhappy.

Down the shadowy road they passed, those two whose lives had met, and mingled, and parted again. Those two so necessary to each other, and who, despite the necessity, must touch hands and part.

'Tis said God makes for every human soul a counterpart, a soul-helper. If this be so, then is it true that every soul must find its counterpart, since God does not work by half, and knows no bungling in His plan. That other self is somewhere,--on this earth, or in some other sphere. The souls are separated, perhaps by death, perhaps by human agency. What of that? Soul will seek soul; will find its counterpart and perform its work, its own half share, though death and vast eternity should roll between.

They passed on, those two, wishing for and needing each the other. Wishing until God heard, and made the wish a prayer, and answered it, in His own time and manner.

At the crossing of the roads where one breaks off to Dan, the mountain preacher's little cabin stood before them.

Nothing, and yet it had a bearing on their lives. On his, at all event.

Before the door, leaning upon the little low gate, an old man with white hair and beard was watching the gambols of two children playing with a large dog. The cabin, old and weatherworn, the man, the tumble-down appearance of things generally, formed a strange contrast with the magnificence of nature visible all around. To Donald, with his southern ideas of ease and elegance, there was something repulsive in the scene. But the woman was more charitable.

"Good evening, parson," she called, "we are going over to Dan to watch the moon rise."

"Yes, yes," said the old man. "An' hadn't ye better leave the gun, sir? There's no use luggin' that to Dan. An' ye'll find it here 'ginst you come back."

"Why, we're going back another route," they told him; not dreaming what that route would be.

"You have a goodly country, parson," said Donald,"and so near heaven one ought to find peace here."

"It be not plentiful," said the old man. "An' man be born to trouble as the sparks go up'ard. But all be bretherin, by the grace o' God, an' bound alike for Canaan."

They passed on, bearing the old man's meaning in their hearts. All bound upon one common road for Canaan.

Oh, Israel! Israel! the wandering in the wilderness goes on. The Promised Land still lies ahead, and wanderers in earth's wilderness still seek it, panting and dying, with none to strike a rock in Horeb.

The Promised Land! what glimpses of that glorious country are vouchsafed, mere glimpses, from those rugged heights, such as were granted him, who, weary with his wanderings' sought Pisgah's top to die.

Sometimes, when the mists are lifted and the sun shines through the rifted clouds, what dreams, what visions, what communion with those whom the angels met upon the mountain! They thought upon it, those two, as they passed on to Dan.

To Dan, through the broad gate artistically set with palings of green and white. Under the sweet old cedars deep down into the heart of the woods, with the solemn mountains rising, grim and mysterious, in the twilight. Down the great bluff where the tinkle of falling water tells of the spring hidden in the dim wood's shadowy heart. The golden arrows of sunset are plucked one by one by the shadow-hands of the twilight hidden in the haunted hemlocks. One star rises above the trees and peeps down to find itself quivering in the dusky pool. A little bird flits by with an evening hymn fluttering in its throat.

They stopped at the foot of the bluff and seated themselves upon a fallen tree, the rifle resting, the stock upon the ground, the muzzle against the tree, between them.

Between them, the loaded rifle. She herself had placed it there. They had scarcely spoken, but words are weak; feeling is strong--and silent. His heart was breaking; could words help that? It was she who spoke at last, nestling closer to him a moment, then quickly drawing back. Her hand had touched the iron muzzle of the gun--it was cold, and it reminded her. She drew her hands together and folded them, palm to palm, between her knees, and held them there, lest the sight of his agony drag them from duty and from honor. She could not bear to look at him, she could only speak to him, with her eyes turned away toward the distant mountains.

"Donald," her voice was low and very steady, "there are so many mistakes made, dear, and my marriage was one of them. But, the blunder having been committed, I must abide by it. And who knows if, after all, it be a mistake? Who can understand, and who dares judge? But right cannot grow from wrong. We part. But I shall not leave you, Donald. Here in the heart of the woods--"

"Don't!" he lifted his face, white with agony. "Your suffering can but increase mine. Go back, dear, and forget. Our paths crossed in vain, in vain. Go back, and leave me to my lonely struggles. I shall miss you, oh, my beloved,--" the words choked him, "forget, forget--"

"Never!" again she moved toward him, again drew back. The iron muzzle had touched her shoulder, warningly. She still held her hands fast clasped between her knees. Suddenly she loosed them; opened them, looked at them; so frail, so small, so delicately womanly as they were. He, too, saw them, the dear hands, and made a motion to clasp them, restrained himself, and groaned. She understood, and her whole soul responded. The old calm was gone; the wife forgotten. It was only the woman that spoke as she slipped from her place beside him, to the ground at his feet; and extended the poor hands toward him.

"Donald, O Donald!" she sobbed. "Look at my hands. How frail they are, and weak, and white, and clean. Aye, they are clean, Donald. Take them in your own; hold them fast one moment, for they are worthy. But oh, my beloved, if they falter or go wrong, those little hands, who would pity their polluted owner? Not you, oh, not you. I know the sequel to such madness. Help me to keep them clean. Help me oh, help me!"

She lifted them pleadingly, the tears raining down her cheeks. She, the strong, the noble, appealing to him. In that moment she became a saint, a being to be worshipped afar off, like God.

"Help me!" She appealed to him, to his manhood which he had supposed dead so long the hollow corpse would scarcely hear the judgment trump.

Her body swayed to and fro with the terrible struggle. Aye, she knew what it was to be tempted. She who would have died for that poor drunkard's peace. But that little mound--that little child's grave on the hill-- "Help me!" She reeled forward and he sprang to clasp her. The rifle slipped its place against the log; but it was between them still; the iron muzzle pointed at her heart. There was a flash, a sharp report, and she fell, just missing the arms extended to receive her.

"O my God!" the cry broke from him, a wild shriek, torn from his inmost heart. "O my God! my God! I have killed her. Alice! oh, speak to me! speak to me before my brain goes mad." He had dropped beside her, on his knees, and drawn the poor face to his bosom. She opened her eyes and nestled there, closer to his heart. There was no iron muzzle between them now. She smiled, and whispered, softly:--

"In the heart of the woods. O Love; O Love!"

And seeing that he understood, she laid her hand upon his bosom, gasped once, and the little hands were safe. They would never "go wrong" now, never. Even love, which tempts the strongest into sin, could never harm them now, those little dead hands.

"In the heart of the woods." It was there they buried her, beside that brokenhearted one whose life went with the tidings from old Shiloh, in the little mountain graveyard in the woods 'twixt Dan and Beersheba.

As for him, her murderer, they said, "the accident quite drove him mad." Perhaps it did; he thought so, often; only that he never called it by the name of accident.

"It was God's plan for helping me," he told himself during those slow hours of torture that followed. There were days and weeks when the very mention of the place would tear his soul. Then the old craving returned. Drink; he could forget, drown it all if only he could return to the old way of forgetting. But something held him back. What was it? God? No, no. God did not care for such as he, he told himself. He was alone; alone forever now. One night there was a storm, the cedars were lashed and broken, and the windows rattled with the fury of the wind. The rain beat against the roof in torrents. The night was wild, as he was. Oh! he, too, could tear, and howl, and shriek. Tear up the very earth, he thought, if only he let his demon loose.

He arose and threw on his clothes. He wanted whiskey; he was tired of the struggle, the madness, the despair. A mile beyond there was a still, an illicit concern worked only at night. He meant to find it. His brain was giving way, indeed. Had already given way, he thought, as he listened to the wind calling him, the storm luring him on to destruction. The very lightning beckoned him to "come and be healed." Healed? Aye, he knew what it was that healed the agonies of mind that physics could not reach. He knew, he knew. He had been a fool to think he would forego this healing. He laughed as he tore open the door and stepped out into the night. The cool rain struck upon his burning brow as he plunged forward into the arms of the darkness. He had gone but two steps when the fever that had mounted to his brain began to cool. And the wind--he paused. Was it speaking to him, that wild, midnight wind?

" 'In the heart of the woods. O Love, O Love!' "

There was a shimmery glister of lightning among the shadowy growth. Was it a figure, the form of a woman beckoning him, guiding him? He turned away from the midnight still, and followed that shimmery light, straight to the little graveyard in the woods, and fell across the little new mound there, and sobbed like a child that has rebelled and yielded. A presence breathed among the shadows; a presence that crept to his bosom when he opened his arms, his face still pressed against the soft, new sod. A strange, sweet peace came to him, such as he had never felt before, filling him with restful, chastened, and exquisite sadness. The storm passed by after awhile, and the rain fell softly-- as the dew falls on flowers. And he arose and went home, with the chastened peace upon him, and the old passionate pain gone forever.

* * * * * * * *

But as the summers drifted by, year after year, he returned. He became a familiar comer to the humble mountain folk, where summer twilight times they saw him leaning on the parson's little gate, conversing with the old man of the "Promised Land" toward which, as "brethren," they were travelling. Sometimes they talked of the blessed dead--the dear, dear dead who are permitted to return to give help to their loved ones.

Aye, he believes it, knows it, for the old temptation assails him no more forever. That is enough to know.

And in the heart of the woods in the dewy twilight, or at the solemn midnight, she comes to meet him, unseen but felt, and walks with him again along the way from Dan to Beersheba. He holds communion with her there, and is satisfied and strengthened.

God knows, God knows if it be true, she meets him there. But life is no longer agony and struggle with him. And often when he starts upon his lonely walks, he hears the wind pass through the ragged cedars with a low, tremulous soughing and bends his ear to listen. "In the heart of the woods, O Love, O Love."

And he understands at last how to those passed on is vouchsafed a power denied the human helper, and that she who would have been his guide and comforter now gave him better guardianship--a watchful and a holy spirit.

Meanwhile, the dead rest well.

CHRISTMAS EVE AT THE CORNER GROCERY.

THE boss had not returned; in truth, the probability was the boss would not return that night, inasmuch as he had generously offered the bookkeeper, who was clerk as well, permisson to go to his supper first. True, the subordinate had declined the honor; it being Christmas eve, Saturday night, close upon the heels of the new year, and the books of the establishment sadly in need of posting. The subordinate did not relish the prospect of a lonely Christmas, Sunday at that, on the tall stool behind the big desk among the cobwebs, mackerel and onion scents, sardine boxes, nail kegs, coils of barbed wire, soap-smelling cotton stuffs, molasses and coal oil. So he gave up his supper, and the half-hour with the cripple (he sighed for the half-hour more than for the supper), contented himself with a bite of cheese and a cracker, which he forthwith entered upon the book, as he had been ordered to do, in a clear, clerical hand: "To S. Riley, cheese and crackers, .07." He wrote it in his best hand, to cover up the smallness of it, perhaps, for it was a very small entry. The subordinate's face wore something very like a sneer as he made it, although he had the consolation of knowing the smallness of the transaction was upon the side of the creditor.

It was a general kind of a store, was the grocery on the corner; a little out of the way, beyond the regular beat of the city folk, but convenient to the people of the suburbs. It wasn't a mammoth concern, although its stock was varied. The boss, the real owner of the establishment, and Riley, the bookkeeper, ran it, without other help than that of black Ben, the porter.

Riley was both bookkeeper, clerk, and, he sometimes suspected, general scapegoat to the proprietor. To-night he was left to attend to everything, for he knew the boss would not leave his warm hearth to trudge back through the snow to the little corner grocery that night. His daughter had come for him in a sleigh, and had carried him off, amid warm furs and the jingle of sleigh-bells, to a cheery Christmas eve with his family.

The bookkeeper sighed as he munched his cheese. There was a little lame girl away up in the attic on Water Street that Riley called home. She would hear the sleighbells go by and peep down from her dingy little window, and clap her hands and wish "daddy would come home for Christmas, too." There wasn't any mother up there in the attic; for out in the cemetery, in the portion allotted to the common people, the snow was falling softly on the little mother's grave.

The clerk ate his cheese in silence. Suddenly he cropped his fist upon the desk heavily. "Sometimes I wish she was out there with her mother," he said. "Sometimes I wish it, 'specially at Christmas times. Let me see: she is ten years old to-night; we called her our 'Christmas gift,' and never a step have the little feet taken. Poor Julie! poor little Christmas snowbird! poor little Christmas sparrow! I always think of her somehow when the boys go by in the holidays with a string of dead birds they've shot. Poor little daughter!"

He sighed, and took up his pen; it was a busy season. A step caused him to look up; then he arose and went to wait upon a customer. It was a woman, and Riley saw that she had been weeping.

"Howdy do, Mrs. Elkins," he said. "What can I do for you?"

115

"I want to know the price of potatoes, Mr. Riley," she replied.

"Sixty cents a bushel. How is the little boy to-night, Mrs. Elkins? Is he getting well for Christmas?"

"Yes," said the woman. "He's already well; well an' happy. I fetched him to the graveyard this mornin'."

Riley dropped the potato he had taken from the tub, and looked up to see the woman's lip quiver.

"What's the price o' them potatoes?"

"Fifteen cents a peck."

She laid a silver dime upon the counter.

"Gimme them many," she said; "there's four more lef' to feed besides the dead one though," she added quickly, "I--ain't be-grudgin' of 'em victuals."

Riley measured a peck of the potatoes, and emptied them into her basket. Four mouths besides her own, and one little starveling left that day, "that blessed Christmas eve," in the graveyard. He found himself hoping, as he went back to the ledger, that they had buried the baby near his own dead. The big graveyard wouldn't feel so desolate, so weirdly lonesome, as he thought it must, to the dead baby if the little child mother, his young wife, could find it out there among all that array of the common dead. "To S. Riley, 1-3 of peck of potatoes, .05." The blue blotter had copied, or absorbed the entry, made it double, as if the debt had already begun to draw interest. The clerk, however, had not noticed the blotter; other customers came in and claimed his attention. They were impatient, too. It was a

116

very busy night, and the books, he feared, would not be balanced after all. It was shabby, downright mean, of the boss not to come back at a time like this.

The new customer was old man Murdock from across the river, the suburbs. He had once been rich, owned a house up town, and belonged to the aristocracy. He had possessed the appurtenances to wealth, such as influence, leisure, at one time. He still was a gentleman, since nature, not circumstance, had had the care of that. Every movement, every word, the very set of the threadbare broadcloth, spoke the proud, the "well-raised" gentleman of the Old-South time. "Good evening, Mr. Riley," he said, when the clerk stumbled down from his perch. The male customers--they learned it from the boss, doubtless--called him "Riley." They generally said, "Hello, Riley." But the old Southerner was neither rude nor so familiar. He said, "Good-evening, Mr. Riley," much the same as he would have said to the president, "Good-evening, Mr. ---- "; and he touched his long, white, scholarly-looking finger to the brim of his hat, though the hat was not lifted. Riley said, "Good evening" back again, and wanted to know "what Mr. Murdock would look at." He would have put the question in the same way had Mr. Murdock still possessed his thousands and he would have put it no less respectfully had the gentleman of fallen fortunes come a-begging. There is that about a gentleman commands respect; great Nature willed it so.

The customer was not hurried; he remarked upon the weather, and thawed himself before the big stove (he never once broached the subject of Christmas, nor became at all familiar), pitied the homeless such a night, hoped it would freeze out the tariff upon wool; then he asked, carelessly, as men of leisure might, "What is the price of bacon, Mr. Riley?--by the hundred."

"Eight dollars a hundred, Mr. Murdock," said Riley.

The ex-millionaire slipped his white fore-finger into his vest pocket. After a moment's silence, during which Riley knew the proud old heart was breaking, though the calm face gave no sign of the struggle, "Put me up a dime's worth of the bacon, if you please."

Riley obeyed silently; he would no more have presumed to cover up the pathos of the proceeding by talk than he would have thought of offering a penny, in charity, to the mayor in the city. He put the transaction as purely upon a business footing as if the customer had ordered a round ton of something. He wrapped the meat in a sheet of brown paper, and received the stately "Good evening, sir," saw the white finger touch the hat brim as the customer passed out into the snow, then climbed back to his perch, thinking, as he did so, that of all poverty the poverty that follows fallen fortunes must be the very hardest to endure. There is the battle against old longings, long-indulged luxuries, past pleasures, faded grandeurs, dead dreams, living sneers, and pride, that indomitable blessing, or curse, that never, never dies. God pity those poor who have seen better days!

"To S. Riley, 2 lbs. bacon, at 12 1-2 cts., .25." The book bore another entry. Riley put the blotter over it very quickly; he had a fancy the late customer was looking over his shoulder. He shouldn't like the old gentleman to see that entry, not by any means.

"Chris'mus gif', marster."

Another customer had entered. Riley closed the big ledger, and thrust it into the safe. The day-book would take up the balance of the evening.

"What can I do for you, Aunt Angie?" he said, going behind the counter to wait upon the old colored woman, who had passed the compliments of the season after the old slave custom.

She laughed, albeit her clothing was in rags, and the thin shawl gathered about her shoulders bore patches in blue and yellow and white.

"I cotched yer Chris'mus gif', good marster; yer knows I did."

"But you're a little early, Aunt Angie," said the clerk; "this is only Christmas eve."

"Aw, git out, marster. De ole nigger got ter cook all day ter-morrer--big Chris-'mus dinner fur de whi' folks. No res' fur de ole nigger, not even et Chris'mus. Bress de Lord, it ain' come but onc't a year."

She laughed again, but under the strange merriment Riley detected the weariness that was thankful; aye, that thanked God that Christmas, the holiday of the Christ-child, came "but once a year."

Christmas! Christmas! old season of mirth and misery! Who really enjoys it, after all? Lazarus in the gutter, or Dives among his coffers?

The clerk ran his eye along the counters, the shelves, and even took in the big barrels, pushed back, in the rear, out of the way.

"Well, Aunt Angie, what shall the 'gift' be?"

He could see the bare toes where her torn old shoes fell away from the stockingless feet. She needed shoes; he was about to go for a pair when she stopped him by a gesture.

"Dem ar things, marster," she said, pointing to a string of masks--gaudy, hideous things, festooned from the ceiling. "I wants one o' dem ar. De chillun'll lack dat sho."

He allowed her to select one; it was the face of a king, fat, jovial, white. She enjoyed it like a child. Then, unwrapping a bit of soiled muslin, she took from it three pieces of silver, three bright, precious dollars. They represented precisely three fourths of her month's wages. She purchased a tin horn "fur de baby, honey"; a candy sheep "fur Ephum, de naix un"; a string of yellow beads "fur Jinny. Dat yeller gal ain' got no reason-mint she am dat set on habin' dem beads"; a plug of tobacco "fur de old man's Christmus"; a jew's-harp "fur Sam; dat chile gwi' l'arn music, he am "; a doll "fur Lill Ria; she's de po'ly one, Lill Ria am"; and last, "a dust ob corn meal ter make a hoe-cake fur dey-all's Chris'mus dinner."

She had been lavish, poor beggar; without stint she had given her all; foolishly, perhaps, but she apologized in full for the folly: "It am Chris'mus, marster."

Aye, Christmas! wear your masks, poor souls; fancy that you are kings, kings. Dream that pain is a myth and poverty a joke. Make grief a phantom. Set red folly in the seat of grim doubt, pay your devoirs one day! To-morrow the curtain rises on the old scene; the wheels grind on; the chariots of the rich roll by, and your throat is choked with their dust; your day is over. The clerk made his entry in the day-book, "To S. Riley, one mask,. 20," before he waited upon three newsboys who were tapping the floor with their boot heels, just in front of the counter.

The largest of the trio took the role of spokesman:--

"I want a pack o' firecrackers, Mister; an' Jim wants one, an' so does Harry. Can't we have 'em all for ten cents?"

The clerk thrust his pen behind his ear.

"They are five cents a pack," he said.

"Can't you come down on three packs? They do up town, an' we ain't got another nickel."

Riley read the keen interest of the transaction in the faces before him. But he had orders. "Couldn't do it, boys, sorry."

"Well, then,"--but a half sigh said it wasn't "well,"-- "give us gum. We can divide that up anyhows."

It was a poor compromise--a very poor compromise. The face, the very voice, of the little beggar expressed contempt. Riley hesitated. "Pshaw!" said he, "Christmas without a racket is just no Christmas to a boy. I know, for I've been a boy, too. And it only comes once a year. Here, boys, take the three packs for ten cents, and run along and enjoy yourselves."

And as they scampered out, he sighed, thinking of two poor little feet that could never throw off their weight and run, as only childhood runs, not even at the Christmas time.

"To S. Riley, 1 pack of firecrackers, .05."

Then it was the clerk took himself to task. He was a poor man on a small salary. He had a little girl to look after, a cripple, who would never be able to provide for herself, and for whom, in consequence, some one else must provide. She would expect a little something for Christmas, too. And the good neighbor in the attic who kept an eye on the little one while Riley was at work--he must remember her. It was so pleasant to give he wondered how a man with a full pocket must feel when he came face to face with suffering. God! if he could feel so once! just once have his pockets full! But he would never be rich; the boss had told him so often: he didn't know the value of a dollar. The head of the establishment would think so, verily, when he glanced over the night's entries in the day-book.

"Oh, well, Christmas comes but once a year!" he said, smiling, as he adopted the universal excuse.

Some one came in and he went forward again.

"No, he didn't keep liquor; he was outside the corporation line and came under the four-mile restriction."

"Just a Chris'mus toddy," said the customer that might have been. "Don' drink reg'lar. Sober's anybody all th' year, cep-- Chris'mus. Chris'mus don't come--don't come but once--year."

He staggered out, and Riley stepped to the door to watch him reel safely beyond the boss's big glass window.

There was another figure occupying the sheltered nook about the window. Riley discovered the pale, pinched little face pressed against the pane before he opened the door. The little waif was so utterly lost in wonder of the Christmas display set forth behind the big panes, that he did not hear the door open or know that he was observed until the clerk's voice recalled his wandering senses.

"See here, sonny, you are marring the glass with your breath. There will be ice on that pane in less than ten minutes."

The culprit started, and almost lost his balance as he grasped at a little wooden crutch that slipped from his numb fingers and rolled down upon the pavement.

"Hello!" The clerk stepped out into the night and rescued the poor prop.

Humanity! Humanity! When all is told, thy great heart still is master.

"Go in there," the clerk pointed to the door, "and warm yourself at the fire. It is Christmas; all the world should be warm at Christmas."

The waif said nothing; it was enough to creep near to the great stove and watch the Christmas display from his warm, safe corner.

"There's that in the sound of a child's crutch strikes away down to my boots," the clerk told himself as he made an entry after the boy had left the store. "Whenever I hear one I--Hello! what is it, sissy?"

A little girl stood at the counter. A flaxen haired, blue-eyed little maiden; alone, at night, and beautiful. Growing up for what?

Crippled feet, at all events, are not swift to run astray. The clerk sighed. The Christmas eve was full of shadows;

shadows that would be lost in the garish day of the morrow. He leaned upon the counter. "What do you want, little one?"

"Bread."

Only a beggar understands that trick of asking simple bread. Ah, well! Christmas must have its starvelings, too! The big blotter lingered upon the last entry. And when he did remove it to go and wait upon some new customers he quieted the voice of prudence with the reflection that his own wee one might stand at a bread counter some pitiless Christmas eve, and this loaf, sent upon the waters of mercy, might come floating back; who could tell since,--and the clerk smiled,--

> " 'The world goes 'round and 'round;
> some go up, and some go down.' "

The counter was crowded; it was nearing the hour for closing, and, business was growing brisk. And some of the customers were provokingly slow, some of the poorer ones keeping the richer ones waiting. It isn't difficult to buy when there is no fear of the funds running short. There was one who bought oysters, fruit, and macaroni, ten dollars, all told, in less than half the time another was dividing twenty-five cents into a possible purchase of a bit of cheese, a strip of bacon, and a handful of dry beans. And old Mrs. Mottles, the shopgirls' landlady at the big yellow tenement, up town a bit, took a full twenty minutes hunting over cheap bits of steak, stale bread, and a roast that "ought to go mighty low, seeing it was toler'ble tough and some gristly." Riley was pretty well tired out when the last one left the store. He glanced at the clock: eleven-ten; he had permission to close at eleven, and it was ten minutes past.

He went out and put up the shutters, came back, and began putting away the books.

The big ledger had scarcely been touched; he had been too busy to post that night.

"Mr. Riley? Mr. Riley? Just a minute before you close up, Mr. Riley."

He went back to the counter, impatiently; he was very tired. A woman with a baby in her arms stood there waiting.

"I am late," she said, "a'most too late. I want a bite for to-morrow. Give me what will go farthest for that."

She laid a silver quarter upon the counter.

"How many of you?" said Riley. "It might make a lunch for one--"

The woman shook her head.

"A drunkard counts for one when it comes to eatin', anyhows," she said, and laughed--a hard, bitter laugh. "He counts for somethin' when he's drunk," she went on, the poor tongue made free by misery that would repent itself on the morrow. "May be man, brute likely. I've got the proofs o' it."

She set the child upon the counter and pushed back her sleeve, glanced a moment at a long, black bruise that reached from wrist to elbow, then quickly lowered the sleeve again.

"Give me somethin' to eat, Mr. Riley, for the sake o' your own wife, sir,--an' the Christmas."

His own wife! Why, she was safe; safe forever from misery like that. He almost shrieked it to the big blue blotter. And then he looked to see what he had written. He almost trembled, lest in his agony he had entered upon the master's well-ordered book his thought: "Safe! Elizabeth Riley under the snow--Christmas," he had written it somewhere, upon his heart, perhaps, but surely somewhere. The entry in the boss's look was all right; it read a trifle extravagantly, however:--

- To S. Riley . . . . Dr.
- 1 shoulder, 10 Lbs.. @10 cents $1.00
- 2 lbs.. coffee @ 30 cents 60
- 2 lbs.. sugar @ 12 1/2 cents 25
- 3 doz. eggs @ 15 cents 45

"For the sake of the dead wife," he told the blue blotter,--"the dead wife and the Christmas time." Then he thrust the book into the safe, turned the combination, looked into the stove, lowered the gas, and went home.

Home to the little attic and the crippled nestling. She was asleep, but a tiny red stocking, worn at the heel, though thoroughly clean, hung beside the chimney.

He tiptoed to the bed, and looked down at the little sleeper. There was a smile upon the baby lips, as if in dreams the little feet were made straight, and were skipping through sunny meadows, while their owner's hand was clasped fast in the hand of the hero of all childish adoration,--the mythical, magical Santa Claus.

The little hands were indeed clasped tightly upon a bit of cardboard that peeped from beneath the delicate fingers, upon the breast of the innocent sleeper. Riley drew it gently away. It was a Christmas card the neighbor-woman had picked up in some home of the rich where she had gone that day to carry home some sewing. It bore a face of Christ, and a multitude, eager, questioning; and underneath a text:--

"Inasmuch as ye did it unto one of the least of these, my brethren, ye did it unto me."

He sighed, thinking of the hungry horde, the fainting multitude at the grocery that Christmas eve.

His heart had ached for them; he understood so well what it was to be wretched, lonely, hungry. Not one of those he had helped had thanked him, in words; not one had wished him a Merry Christmas. Yet, for what he had done, because of it, the little red stocking by the chimney-place would be half empty. He hadn't missed their thanks, poor starvelings, and to, say "Merry Christmas," would have been to mock. Yet he fancied a smile touched for an instant the lips of the pale Nazarene, those lips said to have never smiled, as he slipped the card to its place under the wee hands folded upon the child's heart.

And after a little while he was lying by her side, too tired to sleep, thinking of the unbalanced ledger and the books that must be posted before the year should end.

At last he slept. But the big ledger refused to leave him; even in dreams it followed to annoy, and drag him back to the little suburban grocery. And when he unlocked the safe and took it out, lo! he was surrounded by a host of beggars: boys without money wanting firecrackers; women with starving babies in their arms; little girls crying for bread; old men, young men, white, black,--all the beggars of the big round world. They seized the boss's big book and began to scribble in it, until a little girl with a crutch began to beat them off. And when they were gone he could still hear the noise of them--a mighty rustle of wings; and he saw that they had gathered all about him, in the air; and they no longer begged,--they laughed. And there was one who wore a mask; and when it was removed he saw the face of Christ.

Then he took back his old ledger, and lo! upon the credit side where the balance was not made, a text had been entered. It filled the page down to the bottom line:--

"Inasmuch as ye did it unto the least of these, ye did it unto me."

And full across the page, as plain as if it had been in blood, ran the long red lines that showed the sheet was balanced.

THE END.

www.ingramcontent.com/pod-product-compliance
Lightning Source LLC
Chambersburg PA
CBHW051514260626